*A
Harlequin
Romance*

OTHER

Harlequin Romances

by ANNE WEALE

Many of these titles are available at your local bookseller,
or through the Harlequin Reader Service.

For a free catalogue listing all available Harlequin Romances,
send your name and address to:

HARLEQUIN READER SERVICE,
M.P.O. Box 707, Niagara Falls, N.Y. 14302
Canadian address: Stratford, Ontario, Canada.

or use order coupon at back of book.

A TREASURE
FOR LIFE

by

ANNE WEALE

HARLEQUIN BOOKS   TORONTO
WINNIPEG

Original hard cover edition published in 1972
by Mills & Boon Limited, 17 - 19 Foley Street
London W1A 1DR, England

© Anne Weale 1972

Harlequin edition published October, 1972

SBN 373-01629-8

Printed in Canada

1629

'The evening (29th July 1843) we spent at the sequestered abode of Sophia Würstemberger's parents. There we enjoyed a memorable view of the Bernese Alps covered with snow. Who can describe their magnificence? It is but seldom that the clouds have lately allowed any view of them. We gazed, and gazed, and gazed for about an hour; receiving abundant information, geographical and historical, from our host.
'The picture left on the mind by this mountain range is a treasure for life.'

From the Journal of Joseph John Gurney
of Earlham Hall near Norwich.

CHAPTER I

In the middle of the summer night, Jane opened her eyes and saw, on the white-painted wall, the shadow of a man. The man himself was behind her, climbing through her bedroom window.

She had been dreaming and, for some seconds, this seemed to be part of her dream. Without surprise or alarm, she watched the silent shadow-play. It was only when a cloud hid the moon, and she heard a movement in the darkness, that she was frightened.

Stealthily she reached for the switch of the bedside lamp. Fear made her clumsy, and the lamp was always unsteady, its shade being too large for its base. Instead of turning it on, she knocked it off the table.

Her instinctive reaction to this was to spring out of bed and make a dash for the door. But she was scarcely on her feet when the intruder switched on a torch, and transfixed her with a bright, white beam.

"Good lord! A girl!" he said softly. He sounded surprised, but not unnerved.

His voice made Jane less afraid, for it seemed too calm, and too cultured, to belong to a housebreaker.

"Don't be frightened. I'm not a burglar." When she did not respond to this statement, he repeated it in French, and then in German.

At this she recovered her wits. "Then I'd like to know what you are doing?" she said indignantly.

"I'm David Carleton, Doctor Wroxham's brother-in-law. I was trying to get into the house without waking anyone. I thought this room would be empty, ready for me."

"Well, it isn't," retorted Jane crossly. "Why didn't you *say* you were coming? We would have left the front door unlocked. When you telephoned Mary this morning, you said you were *not* coming home." She bent down to pick up the lamp and replace it on the table.

"I know, but I changed my –"

He stopped as she turned on the light. They stared at each other.

He was not like his sister to look at. He was tall and dark, although his eyes were not deep brown as they should have been to go with his hair and his tan.

However, it was not the un-matching colour of his eyes which caught Jane's attention just then, but rather the expression in them, an expression which made her aware that tonight, by an unlucky chance, she was wearing Bettina's silly nightdress.

The nightdress did not belong to Bettina. It had been a Christmas present from her; one of her periodic attempts to infiltrate a little glamour into Jane's severely serviceable wardrobe.

Ordinarily Jane, now twenty, went to bed in the same sort of pyjamas she had worn when she was twelve. Bettina's nightdress was suitable for a rich girl's trousseau, and extremely unsuitable for a midnight encounter with a man one had never met before. Fortunately Jane had left her dressing-gown lying across the foot of the bed. Blushing, she snatched it up and put it on.

"There's no room ready for you," she said.

"Not to worry; I'll sleep on the couch in the surgery. I've done it before," he said carelessly. "But first I need something to eat. There's some bacon in the house, I hope. I haven't had any decent bacon or cheese since I was last in England."

"I believe there's some streaky," said Jane. "Couldn't you wait until breakfast? You're sure to wake everyone up if you bang about the kitchen."

"I was hoping you'd cook a snack for me, since I've spoiled

8

your beauty sleep anyway," he said, with cheerful effrontery. "It's only two o'clock now. I can't wait another six hours. My last meal was yesterday's lunch."

"What on earth have you been dong since then?"

"Oh, this and that."

Jane remembered what his sister had said after his telephone call announcing his arrival in London. "I expect he's not coming down to Norfolk because he's got some gorgeous girl keeping champagne on ice for him," she had remarked, with a grin and a shrug.

"After such a long time away?" Jane had said doubtfully, knowing that, for the past eighteen months, her employer's brother, who was a mining surveyor, had been in South America.

"Oh, David is the kind of man for whom women seem to enjoy waiting. Goodness knows why. He's not handsome or rich – though he is rather attractive, I suppose."

But perhaps this time the girl had decided that eighteen months was too long to hang about for any man, Jane thought acidly, as she looked across the lamplit bedroom at him. Perhaps this time he had gone through his address book, and every girl he had dated on his last leave was now married, engaged, or merely no longer interested.

It was on the tip of her tongue to say that if he wanted bacon at this hour he would have to cook it himself when it occurred to her that, if she did not do it for him, he was probably selfish enough to wake up his sister. And the reason why Jane was a temporary member of the Wroxham household was to ease Mary Wroxham's domestic burdens.

"Oh, very well," she said stiffly, stepping into her bedroom slippers. On the way past the dressing-table, she picked up the thick rubber band with which, during the day, she kept her shoulder-length hair fastened back from her face.

Downstairs, he said quietly, "I left my car down the road. I'll go and fetch my bags."

By the time he returned, the bacon was sizzling under the

9

grill, coffee was percolating, and Jane was grating some of Doctor Wroxham's favourite extra-strong Cheddar to put in a three-egg omelette.

She had laid a place for him at one end of the large kitchen table where the Wroxhams ate all informal meals. When she had transferred the omelette to a hot plate, arranged the bacon alongside it, and set it before him, she would have said good night and returned to bed.

But he said, "Don't run away. Have a cup of your excellent coffee, and tell me how everyone is, and what you're doing here? I don't know your name."

"Jane Winfarthing. I'm here to help with the children during the whole school holiday, but particularly during a three-week tour on the Continent."

"They're camping again this year, are they? Well, with five kids they haven't much alternative, I suppose. When does the trip start, and where are you heading?"

"We're leaving on August the eighteenth, and there isn't any fixed itinerary."

"The eighteenth ... a week today. That'll suit me very well," he said thoughtfully. "How come you are free during the holidays? You're not still at school yourself, are you?"

"I'm reading History at U.E.A."

"Where?"

"The University of East Anglia."

Now, in the better light of the kitchen, she could see that the colour of his eyes was an unusual dark grey, not the blueish grey of the cobbled beaches at Weybourne and Cley, near where the Wroxhams lived, but the warmer grey of the knapped-flint cottages to be seen all over north Norfolk.

"So? A blue-stocking! But clever enough to camouflage her brains with frilly nighties, and to know that a light hand with an omelette is worth several degrees in the long run," he said, with a mocking gleam.

Probably he intended to flatter her, but he could not have said anything more calculated to rekindle her antagonism. A few moments earlier, having recovered from her fright at the manner of his arrival, she had been ready to revise her pre-conceived opinion of him, based on various remarks made by his sister.

Now, however, it was abundantly clear that the first impression had been correct. He was one of those insufferable men who regarded unmarried women as playthings, and married women as unpaid housekeepers, content to keep the home fires burning while men went about the world doing all the interesting things.

"I gather that, on and off, you have been out of England for some years, Mr. Carleton," she answered. "Times have changed. It's no longer necessary for women to disguise their intelligence; at least not among men of intelligence. It's only the rather dim men who still prefer feather-brained women."

He laughed, making her say, "Hush! You'll wake the others."

"You already have," said a voice from behind them.

"Mary!" He sprang to his feet, and embraced his sister with uninhibited warmth.

Watching their affectionate greetings, sensing the strong bond between them, Jane was conscious of what she had missed by having no close family ties. Her friendship with Bettina Brooke was the nearest she had come to a loving relationship.

"But how did you get in, David?" asked Mrs. Wroxham, when she had recovered from the first surprise and pleasure of his unexpected arrival.

"Through Jane's bedroom window."

"*What?* Oh, really – what a mad thing to do! I'm surprised she didn't scream the place down. Weren't you terrified?" – to Jane.

Before she could answer, David said sardonically, "Times have changed, my dear Mary. Only a feather-brained girl would scream at the sight of a man climbing in at her bedroom window. The intelligent thing to do in such a contingency is to pretend to be soundly asleep. Nowadays, when

11

most housebreakers are panicky amateurs, it's a mistake to take them by surprise. If they're armed, they are liable to shoot one."

"Is that what Jane did? Pretended to be asleep?" asked his sister.

The corners of his mouth quirked. "No, she suddenly leapt out of bed, and it was I who had a nasty turn," he said. "Luckily, I had one leg over the sill by then. Otherwise I might have lost my balance, and you would then have been woken by *my* blood-curdling yell as I fell head first to the ground."

"Which would have served you right," said Mrs. Wroxham. "I hope you've apologised properly. It's very magnanimous of Jane to be making you welcome. You don't deserve it. Actually it was the smell of bacon, not your voices, which woke me."

"If you'll excuse me, I'll go back to bed," said Jane.

Mary Wroxham smiled at her. "Yes, do. Good night, Jane."

Her brother rose to his feet again. "Sleep tight, Jane."

Without looking at him, she murmured "Good night," and left the kitchen. But as she reached the landing she realised that she was now much too wide-awake — and too ruffled! — to fall asleep quickly. She would have to read for a little while; but the book she had been reading earlier she had finished before she went to sleep for the first time that night.

In the Wroxhams' sitting-room, the alcoves on either side of the fireplace were filled with several hundreds of books. Jane decided to return downstairs and choose something new to read. Thus it was that, on her way across the hall, her slippers making no sound on the fitted carpet, she overheard David Carleton saying, "I preferred that pretty little *au pair* you had the last time I was here."

"Helga? Yes, and you weren't the only one," replied his sister, with a soft laugh. "Every unattached male for miles around was dazzled by Helga, and several attached ones, too, I regret to say. They came like wasps to a picnic. But Helga was no help to me. I couldn't rely on her for anything. Jane is

12

most useful and sensible. The children took to her immediately."

"I can imagine her keeping them in order. I had a taste of the schoolmarm manner myself."

"Now, David, that isn't fair. You don't seem to appreciate it, but you must have given the poor girl quite a bad scare. I'm not surprised if she was short with you. Normally, she's a very good-natured person."

At this point Jane became aware that she had no right to be listening to this conversation. Forgetting the errand which had caused her unintentionally to eavesdrop, she hastened back upstairs.

But before she was out of earshot, she heard David say, "Perhaps you're right. I'll reserve judgement until tomorrow."

With no new book to distract her, and her antipathy to David Carleton exacerbated by what she had overheard, Jane knew it was useless to try to sleep yet. She decided to add a page to her letter to Bettina.

Bettina, having no need to support herself during the long vacation, was at her parents' villa in Majorca. She had wanted Jane to accompany her to the island, but although she would have loved to go, Jane had refused the invitation. She knew that Bettina had no intention of studying, and therefore it would be almost impossible for her to do so. Bettina did not need a degree. Jane did. Her future depended on it.

Having described the events of the past half an hour in her small, neat hand, she concluded the postscript with – "But the fly in the ointment is only a temporary one, thank goodness. This time next week we shall be en route for Europe."

Next morning, Jane was woken by a kiss on her cheek from the Wroxhams' youngest son.

"You promised to read to *me* today," he said, when she opened one eye at him.

All the children liked being read to, but the books which pleased the others were far above his head.

"Oh, Thomas – not at ten past seven!" she protested, peering at the clock, and then sinking back on her pillow with a groan which became a laugh as she looked at his round, crestfallen face. "I suppose you've been awake since crack of dawn. All right, up you come."

Thomas scrambled on to the bed, and arranged himself comfortably beside her.

He was almost five, and in September he was starting school. Like Jane, he had never been camping abroad before. The previous summer he had stayed behind with his grandparents.

Presently they were joined by Francesca and Emma. Jane put up a finger to indicate that this was Thomas's story time, and they must not interrupt it. They perched at the foot of the bed. Francesca was rising seven. Emma was nine.

The story was almost finished when John and Edward arrived. Edward was Emma's twin. John would be eleven in October.

"Can we go to the beach, today, Jane?" asked Emma, after Jane had closed the book.

Mary, finding that her holiday helper was a strong swimmer, and – equally important! – that the children were obedient to her, now allowed Jane full charge of her offspring if she herself was unable to join an outing.

Jane said, "We'll see what the weather looks like after breakfast. The forecast wasn't too promising. Oh, no, I forgot – today is your day for the dentist." This meant a visit to Norwich, ten miles away.

"Are you taking us, or is Mummy?"

"Can we look round Woolworths?"

"Can we go to the Castle Museum?"

"Can we have fish and chips in the van, like we did last time?"

"I don't know. We'll see," said Jane, laughing at their clamour. "It's time we were all washed and dressed. You too, Thomas, my dumpling."

14

"Why do you call me your dumpling, Jane?"

"Because dumplings are a traditional Norfolk dish – delicious to eat, I'm told – and people who were born in this county are sometimes called Norfolk dumplings. You were born in Norfolk, Thomas." Unable to resist his cuddliness, she gave him a quick hug before pushing him gently off the bed, with instructions to be sure to brush his teeth well.

Later, she heard him saying importantly to Edward, "I was born in Norfolk."

"We all were, silly."

For Jane, life with the Wroxhams was full of small, unfamiliar delights. She had always lived among modern, mass-produced things, and had not discovered the pleasure of being surrounded by old, craftsman-made pieces of furniture. The Wroxhams' possessions were not valuable antiques. Like the walnut chest of drawers in Jane's bedroom, many of their furnishings bore the small scuffs and scars of several generations of use in more than one household.

But every morning, when Jane opened the drawers of the chest, the sight of the markings on the locks – the letters V.R. surmounted by a tiny crown – gave her a curious sense of continuity and security. It amused and warmed her to realise that these smooth-sliding, roomy drawers which now held the tights, bras and briefs of the 1970s had once contained the boned corsets, combinations and open-legged unmentionables of the 1890s.

Of all the charming old pieces which Mrs. Wroxham had found at country sales and in curio shops, the one which Jane liked particularly was the Georgian apothecary box which now contained Mary's cosmetics. It was beautifully made of mahogany, and fitted with many small drawers. But because it lacked the original bottles, it had cost only a few pounds.

As well as introducing Jane to the enjoyment of old furniture, Mary Wroxham had also kindled her interest in needlework. The house was full of beautiful examples of many different forms of embroidery. The chairs in the dining-room

15

had canvas work seats. The twilled linen curtains in the little girls' room were embellished with squirrels, snails, caterpillars and butterflies in Jacobean work. Thomas's bedspread was a copy, in appliqué work, of a Richard Scarry illustration.

But it was not until Jane had been with the family for several days that it dawned on her that all these things had been created by Mrs. Wroxham. "I can't think how you find the time," she remarked, when she had found this out.

"Haven't you noticed anything strange about this household?" asked Mary, smiling. "We have no television. We're not in thrall to the Box – and never will be, while I have any say in the matter. We did have a set for a short time. It was a second-hand one, and after some months it broke down. We came to our senses, and vowed never to buy another. I don't think I'm particularly cranky, but that is a bee in my bonnet. It may be a godsend to invalids, but otherwise I think television is the most appalling waste of time which can be spent in a hundred more interesting and satisfying ways. Do you agree? Or do you think I'm a bit dotty?"

"No, not at all dotty," said Jane. "I think you're wise, especially with children in the house. I –" She had been going to say, "I had to study for my A levels in a freezing bedroom because my stepfather was a television addict." Instead, she asked, "What are you making now?" While they had been talking, Mary had been stitching beads on a piece of silk stretched on a tambour.

"This is for the top of a tights box for my sister-in-law for next Christmas. I try to make all my presents. It's so much cheaper than buying them."

"And much nicer for the people who receive them," Jane had remarked.

Of all the rooms in the Wroxhams' sunny Queen Anne house, the one which Jane liked best was the kitchen. When she ran downstairs, on the morning she was woken by Thomas, the milkman was leaving eight pints on the back doorstep. Jane put the bottles in the big refrigerator, and drew back the

16

crisp gingham curtains. Then she put the pots of geraniums, which had spent the night on the drainers of the stainless steel sink, back in their day-time places on the wide, tiled window-sills.

In the centre of the kitchen, two tables with pine-patterned Formica tops were placed end to end and surrounded by eight Windsor chairs of the kind called 'smoker's bow'. These, Mary had de-varnished, waxed, and cushioned with patch-work.

Jane laid one table, and filled five blue bowls with cereal. She put pots of Israeli honey, peanut butter and peach pre-serve on the revolving tray in the centre of the table, and she washed and refilled the butter dish, and switched on the grill to make toast. By eight o'clock, the children's breakfast was in progress.

Mrs. Wroxham, coming down in her housecoat, walked round the table, admiring her morning-clean offspring.

"My goodness, I never saw such immaculate children. Every ear spotless, every head properly brushed. How do you manage it, Jane? You never seem to shout at them like I do."

"By frightful threats," said Jane, straight-faced. "They know I'm more ruthlesss than you are." She reminded Mary about the appointment with the dentist.

"Yes, and I must also buy the various new bits of uniform which John and the twins need for next term. It's no use put-ting it off until we get back from abroad," said Mrs. Wrox-ham.

Her husband strolled into the kitchen, scanning the head-lines on the front page of the *Eastern Daily Press*. He bade Jane good morning, and added, "I hear you had a disturbed night."

"Yes." Until that moment she had forgotten there was a newcomer in the house.

"Were you sick?" asked Francesca sympathetically.

Before Jane could explain, Doctor Wroxham winked at her. He said to his wife, "By the way, Mary, there are five parcels in the hall. Did you know? They appear to be for the children, but I don't know where they can have come from. It isn't anyone's birthday, is it?"

"Parcels? For us?" cried the twins in unison. They led the dash to the hall.

"But who is it from, Mummy?" asked Emma, examining with mingled pleasure and puzzlement the pogo stick which she had found in her parcel.

Her twin also had a pogo stick, John had a box of Meccano and Francesca, who also liked making things but whose fingers were less deft, had a Bilofix outfit. Thomas needed the assistance of his father to unfasten his parcel. It proved to contain a dozen Ladybird books.

"They're from your Uncle David," explained Mary Wroxham. "You remember he rang me up yesterday from London Airport. Well, now he's here to stay with us for a week. He arrived very late last night."

"But I expect John is the only one who remembers me," said David Carleton, from the top of the stairs.

Evidently he had left the parcels in the hall on his way to his sister's bathroom to shower and shave. He was wearing a navy bath-robe, with what the children called "rubber slipper-sloppers" on his bare brown feet.

As he came down to shake hands with Doctor Wroxham, and re-introduce himself to the small fry, Jane slipped back to the kitchen to get on with clearing the children's things from the breakfast table.

She had noticed that the presents had been bought at Hamleys' toy-shop in London, so evidently not all David's time there yesterday had been spent in pursuit of his own pleasures.

Presently, coming into the kitchen, Mary said, "Jane, as David has a hired car, and is willing to fit in with our arrangements, I think it would be a splendid idea if you and he took care of the tinned stores this morning while I take the children to the dentist. Then we can all meet for lunch, and David has volunteered to take the children round the Castle while I have

18

my hair set for the Plumsteads' dinner party tonight. That will leave you free for a browse in the Central Library, or whatever else you want to do."

It was a plan which filled Jane with dismay, for the last thing she wanted to do was to spend the morning alone with David Carleton. Not that hurrying round Woolworths and Sainsburys. buying the hundred-and-one provisions on Mary's list, would give him much opportunity to bait her. It was the twenty-minute drive to the city that she would have avoided if she could.

"We shan't be going anywhere grand for lunch, shall we?" she asked. "I was thinking of going as I am" – glancing down at her navy jumper and needlecord jeans.

"Oh, no, there's no need to dress up. I expect we shall have fish and chips at that place the children like so much. If David wants to pamper his tastebuds, he can do it later on. When we start our holiday. he's going to motor down to Provence."

Her brother, dressed now, came into the kitchen. "Good morning. I hear I'm to have the pleasure of escorting you round the supermarkets," he said to Jane.

"Yes, if you take the shopping trolley, Jane, and David carries the big tartan grip, you can get it all done in half the time it would take you single-handed," said Mary, sparing Jane the necessity of replying to his remark.

"What would you like for breakfast, Mr. Carleton?" she asked.

She dealt with breakfast, and the children's high tea, and Mary cooked lunch and the adults' evening meal.

"You're very formal," he remarked. "I notice you call my sister Mary." Mrs. Wroxham had left them alone together. "Why not use my first name? I don't intend to call you Miss Winfarthing."

"All right. What would you like to eat . . . David?"

"Some more bacon, if there's any left. But I can cook it myself. I expect you want to get ready to go to Norwich."

"I'm ready now but I ought to see that the children are
19

getting ready. If you're sure you can manage?"

"I should hope so" he said, rather dryly.

Jane escaped into the garden where the twins were striving to master the art of pogo-jumping.

"It's terribly difficult, Jane. You have a go."

"I'd like to try later, Edward. But now you must change into your good clothes."

At home the children wore what their mother called "unisex hand-me-downs", meaning blue jeans, tee-shirts and jerseys which were passed from John to the younger children until they were beyond repair. For going out, they had clothes of their own which Mary made for them.

When Jane had first met Mary, she had been astonished that this slender, fashionable, animated woman was the wife of a country doctor and the mother of five children. Living with Mary had made Jane realise, for the first time, that running a home was not necessarily monotonous and soul-destroying. She had begun to see that, as Mary practised it, housekeeping could be a career as exacting, and as fulfilling, as any other profession. But this discovery had not weakened her conviction that every woman should have a way of supporting herself.

No one knew better than Jane that all marriages were not as happy as the Wroxhams'; and that, when a marriage was not happy, but the couple were held together by the total dependence of the wife, the result was misery for everyone involved. It was because she was the offspring of such a marriage, and for years had been torn in two by conflicting loyalties, that Jane was fiercely determined never to be caught in that trap herself. If, many years ahead, she did marry, it would be on terms of complete equality.

"But what about falling in love? How will you resist?" Bettina had asked, during one of their discussions on marriage.

"I don't think I'm particularly susceptible, and I know I'm not specially attractive, so it isn't likely that a mutual attraction will happen very often," Jane had answered. "If it does, I shall just have to steel myself against it. The thing is to get safely through one's late teens and early twenties when the instinct to perpetuate the species is very strong. By the age of, say, twenty-eight, that urge is dying to some extent. One can choose a partner for rational reasons."

"But by then all the best men will have been snapped up – like summer clothes if one doesn't shop for them in April," Bettina had argued.

Privately, she thought her friend was extremely attractive. But not many people noticed the fact because Jane seemed to take as much care to make herself seem dull and dowdy as Bettina did to look alluring.

Soon after nine, Mary and the children set out for Norwich in the blue Ford Transit van which, next week, the Wroxhams, and Thomas, would use as a mobile bedroom, while Jane and the other four children slept under canvas.

"I expect you find it rather cold here compared with Peru," Jane said politely, as she and David followed on in his hired car.

It was a cool, dull morning, but she was warm enough in her Shetland jumper, whereas he, she noticed, was wearing a much thicker sweater under a raincoat.

"Yes, it takes a few days to become acclimatised. What part of the world do you come from?"

When people asked her this, Jane always answered "London", although in the old-fashioned sense of belonging to a place by virtue of being born and having a parental home there, she did not come from anywhere.

On hearing her customary answer, David glanced at her with some surprise. "As near as that? I assumed that, as you're here for the whole vacation, your family were overseas somewhere."

No doubt he was thinking what his sister, very tactfully, had said: that it seemed rather strange for Jane not to want to spend some part of the summer with her own people.

Jane repeated the explanation she had given to Mary. "My father is dead and my mother has married again. Her husband

21

has some children of his own. It isn't fair to expect him to support someone of my age. It's up to me to earn my own keep."

It was, of course, only a partial explanation. But Mary had accepted it. Probably what she had read between the lines was that Jane and her stepfather did not get on with each other.

This was so; but not for the common reason that Jane was jealous of him, or he of her. For her mother's sake, she had been glad about the marriage; hopeful that, with her second husband, her parent would find the contentment she had never enjoyed with Jane's father.

It had been Richard Kirstead who had brought about the breach between himself and his stepdaughter. He was a prosperous man, and the addition of a young girl to his household – he had two grown-up sons – was not a strain on his income. In any case, his second marriage had saved him the expense of the housekeeper whom he had employed since the death of his first wife. Yet, from the outset, he had fretted over the fact of Jane still being at school in her seventeenth year, which was when the marriage had taken place. When she had dared to tell him that she wanted to go on to a university, his annoyance had been so extreme that he had gone to see her headmistress, and returned, triumphant, with the information that Jane was by no means as clever as she seemed to imagine.

In fact what the Principal had said was that, although Jane was not one of her brilliant pupils, the girl had exceptional powers of concentration and self-discipline, and these qualities should enable her to achieve her ambitions.

The outcome of their clash of wills was that Richard Kirstead had not only refused to make up that part of her State grant deducted by the education authority on account of his high income level, but he had also made it clear that Jane need not expect to find free board and lodging under his roof during the vacations.

But by far the most hurtful part of all this unpleasantness had been the lack of support from her mother. Far from being proud of Jane's achievement, Mrs. Kirstead had agreed with her husband that three years at university was an expensive waste of time.

"How did my sister find you?" David asked.

"She put a card up in a Norwich bookshop where the customers are mainly students. Which reminds me, I must get some books for the journey," she murmured, half to herself.

"What are you going to do after you graduate?" he asked. "Have you decided on a career yet?"

"I'm going to be an archivist. I shall have to take a postgraduate course in archive administration, and then I shall try for a provincial post. In Government departments like the Public Record Office and the British Museum, an Assistant Keeper starts on a higher salary scale, but there are far fewer openings. Besides, I don't want to live in London again."

"Minding a Corporation's minute books seems rather a stuffy occupation for a girl."

"I daresay most occupations seem dull if one doesn't know much about them. There's a good deal more to it than minding minute books."

"That was merely a figure of speech. I don't doubt the interest of the work. But what about the people you will work with? What about the male archivists? I should have thought they tended to be rather desiccated types, or is that also a false impression?"

"I don't know. I haven't met any."

"Wouldn't it be wise to remedy that omission?" he suggested, with a quizzical glance at her. "You don't want to find that you're on the shelf with the archives."

"Heaven forfend!" said Jane ironically. Then, in case he took her exclamation seriously, she added, "Marriage is not the only goal for girls now, you know, and unmarried women are no longer thought of as poor old maids."

At this point David stopped the car to pick up an elderly country woman who, having missed her bus, had been diffidently thumbing a lift by the roadside. She started chatting

23

as soon as she had settled herself behind them, and she did not stop until David dropped her close to the city bus station where she was meeting her sister.

"What a talker!" he said, as they continued on their way.

"I thought she was a dear old thing," said Jane, who liked listening to the accents of deep Norfolk, and for whom the woman's monologue had been greatly preferable to the conversation which had preceded it. Now they had only a few minutes' drive to the car park.

"Anyone would think you were trekking to Outer Mongolia," remarked David when, more than an hour later, Jane ticked the last item off Mary's long list of camping supplies.

"Your sister says that all these things are more expensive abroad, and some of them aren't obtainable. She told me that on the trip last summer they missed English biscuits and chewy sweets."

As they returned to the car with the final load, he said, "Yes, most people in this country don't realise how lucky they are to have such a variety of foods at such reasonable prices. Every time I come back from abroad, it takes me some time to adjust to the prosperity here."

"Do you have to work overseas, or do you prefer it?"

He closed the boot of the car, and pocketed the key. "Let's go and have coffee at the Assembly House, and I'll tell you that, and the story of my life as well, if you like."

Jane had been in the Assembly House, a beautiful eighteenth-century building where concerts, debates and other meetings were held, only once before. They passed through the elegant hall with its lofty ceiling and chandelier to the coffee room. But when they were seated at a corner table, it was not of himself that David began to talk.

He said, "So marriage isn't high among your ambitions? Are you one of these advanced young women who prefers a variety of lovers to the monotony of one husband?"

"No, I am not," she said stiffly.

"Only one lover, perhaps?"

24

To her vexation, she felt herself flushing. "I didn't say that I was anti-marriage, merely that nowadays a woman's life isn't blighted if she doesn't marry. It's possible to be happier with an absorbing career than with a mediocre marriage."

"So I've heard. But, in my observation, the kind of women who are absorbed by a career to that extent are fairly cold-blooded anyway. I should have thought the thing to aim at was a combination of career and home-life."

"Unfortunately it's usually only your sex who can manage to have their cake and eat it," Jane answered. "In *my* observation, after marriage it's always the woman who is expected to run the domestic side of things as well as her own work. If one of the children goes down with measles, for example, it's never the father who takes time off to nurse it. It's always the mother who has to cope. There's a long way to go before there's real equality between men and women."

"Or even between women and women," said David sardonically. "You're luckier than most of the girls in the world, you know. You can choose your own husband, not have him chosen for you. You may have to nurse your children when they're ill, but you won't have to have a baby every year of your life, starting in your early teens. You won't be considered a failure if you don't produce any sons. You may not realise it, but you're in a superior position to most men in the world. You're literate and well fed."

"A typically masculine argument! Of course I realise that I was lucky to be born in England in 1950, instead of 1900 or somewhere where, even now, women are still only chattels. But you can't put a brake on the progress of people in the most advanced countries until people in the least civilised countries have caught up with them."

"I doubt if the further emancipation of Western women would be an advance." He glanced at his watch. "We have an hour to spare before we're due to meet the others. How about going to this bookshop you mentioned earlier? I could do with some paperbacks myself."

"Yes, if you like," she said doubtfully. "But they don't have a very good selection of popular fiction. They specialise in classics and non-fiction."

His grey eyes narrowed a little. "We mining surveyors are a rough crowd, but some of us have been known to struggle through a serious book occasionally."

"I didn't mean to imply that. It was just that I thought you might prefer something light for your holiday. I imagine you're a B.Sc., aren't you?"

"By the skin of my teeth," he agreed negligently.

As they were leaving the coffee room, a girl sauntered out of one of the side rooms where a local artist was having a show. She glanced towards them, and her face lit up with pleasure. "David! When did you get back?"

"Hello, Harriet. You're looking very well. Is that outfit the latest fashion?"

"Well, it hasn't swept Norfolk yet, but it will as soon as the summer holidays are over, and people start to think about their winter clothes," she told him. She was wearing a red linen midi skirt with a white blouse with leg-o'-mutton sleeves. Her waist was cinched by a wide belt, and the slim legs were laced inside high-heeled boots of soft red suede.

"I like it. It's feminine ... suits you," said David approvingly. "Jane, this is Harriet Martham. Jane is helping Mary with the kids for a few weeks," he explained to the other girl.

"Hello." Harriet's mouth smiled while her eyes made a comprehensive appraisal of Jane's appearance. Turning back to David, she said, "I've come in for coffee. Have you had some?"

Jane said quickly, "Why don't you have another, David? I'm sure you two must have lots to talk about. I'll see you later. Good-bye" – this to Harriet.

The fruit and vegetable market next to the ancient flint Guildhall was a short cut to her destination. As she threaded her way down a crowded alley between two rows of stalls, Jane found herself wondering if Harriet Martham was one of those about whom Mary Wroxham had said, "David is the

26

kind of man for whom women seem to enjoy waiting."

Older than she looked from a distance, possibly twenty-six or seven, Harriet was extremely attractive. She would not be single for lack of proposals, but because the one man she cared about was elusive. That man could be David. She had really begun to sparkle after she noticed him. Before, she had looked rather forlorn.

Perhaps seeing her in the new midi look, a fashion which somehow combined an appearance of great modesty with a hint of underlying naughtiness, would revive his interest in her. In the short time that they had stood talking, Jane had sensed intuitively that, at some stage of their lives, David and Harriet had been on close terms with each other.

Somewhat to her surprise, David was not absent from, or even late at, the family rendezvous. He spent the afternoon with the children, as he had promised, and they drove home in his car.

"Did you have a nice afternoon? Did you meet any of your U.E.A. friends?" asked Mary, as she and Jane drove back together.

"No, I didn't. But your brother met a friend this morning. Someone called Harriet Martham."

"Oh, really? She's a pretty creature, isn't she? And she has a terrific flair for clothes. She runs a boutique. It's in quite a small, out-of-the-way village, but people go there from all over the county because her things are so nice, and not too expensive. What was she wearing today?"

Jane described Harriet's outfit.

"David was at school with her brother," said Mary. "There was a time . . . oh, do look at that idiot in front!" – this as a particularly stupid example of selfish driving took place on the road ahead of them. Perhaps she forgot whatever she had started to say, or perhaps she had interrupted herself deliberately, the roadhog providing a convenient means of avoiding an indiscretion. For the rest of the journey she talked about fashion.

27

For the Plumsteads' dinner party that night, she wore a silk jersey trouser suit which made Jane feel a sudden up-surge of the longing for nice clothes which, most of the time, she was able to suppress. The trouble was that, in spite of the age gap between them, in matters of taste she and Mary were very much on the same wavelength. Bettina's ever-changing wardrobe was expensive and fashionable, but too flamboyant to arouse Jane's covetousness often. Mrs. Wroxham dressed in precisely the simple, casual style which Jane hoped to emulate when, several years hence, her career was safely established.

Soon after the Wroxhams left the house, David also went out. He did not say where he was going, or when he would be back, and Jane assumed he would be late. As she was oc-cupying the only spare bedroom, tonight he was going to sleep on an airbed in John's room. After John had gone to bed at half past eight, with permission to read until nine, Jane de-cided to have a shampoo. Mary allowed her to use her hand-dryer, so it was not long before her hair was dry again. Before she replaced the elastic band, she studied herself in the mirror on her bedroom wall.

Was it only friendly flattery, she wondered, when Bettina said that, if she used some make-up and dressed less drably, she could be one of the most attractive girls at U.E.A.?

But I mustn't try to be attractive because then *I* might be attracted to someone, she thought. While nobody is interested in me, it isn't too hard to keep my emotions in cold storage.

She was going downstairs when John came out of his room, and said, "Can I have something to eat? I'm starving."

"All right, as long as you clean your teeth again."

In the kitchen, she fed him with buttered currant bread, and made hot chocolate for both of them. They were drinking it, talking about the camping trip, now only five days away, when they heard a car draw up on the gravel sweep. Jane went to answer the door, but it was not a caller. It was David.

"I only went down to the Swan for a beer," was his response to her surprise that he should have returned so early. As he

28

followed her to the kitchen, he said, "I like your hair better as it is now. It's too severe, pulled back in the horse-tail arrangement."

She had forgotten that her hair was still unbound. Taking the band from her pocket, she put it on. "It gets in my way when it's loose. It becomes untidy."

"There's a poem about that," said David. "Something about a certain disorder in a girl's appearance being more bewitching 'than when art is too precise in every part.' I forget who wrote it, but I agree with him."

"Robert Herrick," Jane said crisply. "But I think it's a foolish poem. To go about with 'a careless shoe-string' is inviting an accident."

"What a down-to-earth young thing you are," he said derisively, stretching forward to open the kitchen door for her. He paused with his hand on the knob, so that Jane could not pass unless she pushed past. "Nevertheless you looked very engaging last night, in that frilly thing, with your hair loose and rather tousled."

Ignoring this, she said coolly, "John is in the kitchen, and it's high time he was in bed."

It incensed her that, although David didn't think much of her compared with the girl called Helga who had been part of the household during his last leave, he was prepared to flirt with her. Probably he flirted with all women, in the same way that if he encountered a dog he would automatically pat it.

It was an attitude she detested, for it seemed to her so derogatory to assume that women were always pleased and flattered by any attention from any man. The reverse of the medal was Bettina's cynical belief that the man did not exist who was proof against the age-old feminine technique of encouraging him to talk about himself, listening with rapt attention to his wafflings, however uninteresting, and never, but never contesting his infallible male opinions.

"I wouldn't want a man who could be won over as easily as that," Jane had said, during one of their many discussions

29

about men in general, and Bettina's current swain in particular. "I think men and women should respect each other, and be sincere and straightforward."

As she shepherded John upstairs, having said good night on her own account, she thought that she would have liked David better had he treated her with honest indifference.

Inevitably the camping trip preoccupied all their minds as the day of departure drew nearer.

"Can we buy some more haggle-slaggle in Holland, Mummy?" asked Francesca, at lunch the next day.

"I expect so, darling."

"What's haggle-slaggle?" asked David.

"Oh, that's the children's name for it. Francesca means *hagel*, the chocolate vermicelli which seems to be a Dutch alternative to marmalade. They almost always put a jar on the breakfast table, as well as jam, and the children like it so much, sprinkled on bread and butter, that at the end of last year's jaunt we bought two big packets to bring home," Mary explained.

"I must try it some time." He turned to his brother-in-law. "So you haven't a fixed route this time? You're going to follow your noses."

"More or less," agreed Doctor Wroxham. "We're definitely going to have a look at the Black Forest in Germany, and our turning point, so to speak, will be the Tal der Wässerfalle in Switzerland."

"What does Tal der What'sit mean, Dad?" John asked.

"Valley of Waterfalls." Speaking to David again, the doctor went on, "One of my patients went there a couple of years ago, and he says it's a glorious spot, and a splendid centre for day-trips. We shall probably spend the whole of our second week there."

"I shouldn't think Jane will care for Switzerland,' said David, looking across the table at her, a hint of laughter in his eyes.

30

"Why on earth not?" asked Mary.

"Haven't you discovered that she's a fanatical feminist? In Switzerland only men have the franchise." Seeing that John wanted to ask something, but couldn't because his mouth was full, David added, "The right to vote at elections."

"They have it now," said Mary. "They were given it while you were away."

John, having swallowed, could speak. "What's a feminist?"

"A person who believes that women are as good as men, if not better," his uncle informed him. "The majority of feminists are rather large, fierce females who think the world will never be put to rights until all the Prime Ministers and Presidents are women."

"Jane is tall, but she isn't fierce," said Emma.

"Not at present," he agreed. "But I expect she will be in later life if she doesn't reform her views."

"Uncle David is joking. Pay no attention to him," said her mother. "A feminist is someone who thinks men and women are equal."

"Are they?' asked Edward.

"No!" said his uncle decisively.

"No," agreed Doctor Wroxham.

"Oh, really, Peter –" Mary began to protest.

"Men and women are different," the doctor continued mildly. "Some men are superior to some women, and vice versa. They're equal only in the sense that both sexes are entitled to the same opportunities in life. Would you agree with that, Jane?"

"Yes," she said, with a smile.

"I didn't realise you were a feminist, Jane," said Mary. "Your generation seems to have achieved complete equality. Or are you fighting now for women in other parts of the world?"

"I'm not a militant feminist," said Jane. "I do have strong views on the subject, but the only time I get a bit hot under the collar is when I meet a dyed-in-the-wool *anti*-feminist."

31

At this point Emma changed the subject by saying suddenly, "Daddy, could we go to see Baron Bomburst's castle in Vulgaria? I thought it was only a make-believe place, but there's a picture of it in Mummy's new book. Oh, do say we can! I'd rather go there than anywhere."

"Baron Whose castle?" her father repeated blankly. "What are you talking about, Emma?"

"She means the castle in 'Chitty Chitty, Bang Bang'," explained Mrs. Wroxham. "But I think it was only a film set, dear, not a proper castle."

"It wasn't. It was real. I'll show you." Emma slipped off her chair and ran from the room. She returned with a copy of a travel guide to Germany which Mary had collected in Norwich, and the paperback "book of the film". This belonged to John who had bought it with a book token after they had been taken to see the film for his birthday treat.

"She's quite right. The castle obviously *is* a real one. It's one of mad Ludwig's castles in Bavaria, not far from Munich," said Mary, having compared two illustrations. "Perhaps we could go to see it, if it isn't too far out of our way."

"The thing I most want to do," said Edward, "is to ride in a cable car. A boy at school was telling us about a story he saw on television about a cable car. There were all these people in it, and something went wrong, and they were stuck half way between two mountains in a terrific storm, and one of the passengers was a murderer ..."

As he paused for breath, his father said dryly, "Your mother would love an experience like that. It would be the highlight of the holiday."

On Sunday, little more than forty-eight hours before their departure, one of Doctor Wroxham's partners, Doctor Swanton, was rushed to hospital after a heart attack. He was a man in his middle forties, apparently in sound health, so everyone was very shocked and anxious. The third partner in the group practice, Doctor Cringleford, was an old man who was waiting for his grandson to qualify before he retired.

At first the Wroxhams' only concern was for their stricken colleague and his wife. It was John who asked, "Does this mean we shan't be able to go camping, Mum?"

"I don't know, dear. We'll have to see," she answered absently.

But later, when the children were in bed, she and her husband discussed the matter.

"I can't possibly leave Matthew Cringleford to cope single-handed for three weeks," said Doctor Wroxham. "Do you think you and Jane can manage the trip without me? The only alternative is to cancel it. The children will be terribly disappointed, but it can't be helped."

"Would it be easier to take them camping in this country?" suggested Jane. "At least there wouldn't be any language problem."

Doctor Wroxham had been the only member of the expedition who spoke some German. Jane's French was quite good, and Mary had a smattering of Spanish, but neither of them knew more than half a dozen words in German, which would cause difficulties if they wanted to explore the more remote parts of the Black Forest where few people would understand English.

"Yes, it would be easier in that respect. I wonder if the ferry company would refund our fares at this late date?" Mary pondered, with a troubled expression. "It's a lot of money to lose if they won't. Oh, dear, I don't know what's best. Even in this country one really needs a man in the party in case of emergencies."

"I'm sure Jane would disagree, but if you feel a man is necessary, how about me?" said her brother.

"You? But you have your own plans, David."

"None that can't be changed."

"I must admit that I should feel happier knowing David was with you, my love," said Doctor Wroxham.

Jane's heart sank. Peter Wroxham was such a nice, easy-going, comfortable sort of man. She had been looking forward,

33

almost as much as his wife and children, to his being with them all day, instead of, as now, only at meal-times. But the prospect of three weeks in the company of his brother-in-law, and in conditions of even closer propinquity than at present, turned her happy anticipation of the holiday to apprehension.

Comfortable was the last word anyone would apply to David Carleton, she thought, glancing at his dark, arrogant profile.

Mary, for a different reason, was as unwilling as Jane for her brother to take her husband's place. She felt that a family camping expedition would be a very tame holiday for a bachelor who had planned more sophisticated diversions.

However, in the end, the two men convinced her that it was the best solution to the problem. It was possible that Doctor Wroxham would be able to obtain a locum for the second half of the holiday. In that event, he would fly out to join his family, wherever they were by that time, and David would then be free to "seek the fleshpots" as his sister put it.

The matter settled, Jane retired to her room to work. It was a lovely warm August evening, but she resisted the temptation to lean on her windowsill and gaze at the peaceful view of fields and woodland. Presently, the deepening twilight caused her to switch on the lamp, and soon moths began to fly in through the wide open casement. Unwilling to close the window on such a soft night, she tried instead to close her mind to their flutterings. But when one velvet-winged creature, after resting on the page she was reading, went blundering back to the lamp, seemingly bent on self-destruction, she felt obliged to save it, first by extinguishing the hot bulb, and then manoeuvring the insect on to her book and transporting it to the window.

It seemed reluctant to take flight. She shook the book to shift it and, in doing so, dislodged a piece of paper from between the leaves. As it floated out of reach, she recognised some notes she had mislaid but did not wish to lose. They came to rest on the flat roof of the surgery block, accessible from the window of the little girls' bedroom.

She recovered her notes without disturbing Francesca and Emma by switching on their light, or making any noise. Passing Francesca's bed, she paused, stirred by an upsurge of tenderness at the sight of the sleeping child. She thought how lucky they were to have been born into a home where the atmosphere of affection and harmony was as pervasive as the scents of cleanliness. Somehow, perhaps because they were such warm-hearted little things themselves, the children often evoked the warmth deep down in Jane's nature.

"Is it really necessary to take little Miss Pankhurst on this trip?"

"Do you mean Jane? Oh, David, that's rather unkind. What have you got against the poor child?"

The voices came from the landing. They were the lowered tones of people mindful that children are sleeping nearby, but the words could be heard with perfect clarity by anyone caught, as Jane was, inside the half open door of the bedroom nearest to the staircase.

"My dear Mary, however useful she may be to you, you must admit she's even more heavy going than the usual run of academic females."

"Does her dig about anti-feminists rankle?" Mary sounded as if there were a twinkle in her eyes.

"I admit to being an anti-feminist if she is an example of the effect of higher education on girls. It's curious how these latterday suffragettes always seem to have a Victorian attitude to sex."

"David! Surely you haven't tried to kiss her?" Mary's tone was startled, and tinged with displeasure.

"For Pete's sake! What do you take me for? I may have spent a longish spell in the wilds, but I haven't yet reached the stage when no female, however frumpish, is safe with me. I'd have to have been overseas for eighteen *years* to find your Miss Pankhurst irresistible."

"Then what did you mean about her attitude to sex?"

"She can't relax if there's a man around. She must find life rather tense at the University, but I suppose a lot of the male students are too busy setting each other's hair and swopping neck chains to be much of a worry to her."

"You're out of touch, my dear," was Mary's reply. "In spite of the way they dress, I've no doubt the young men Jane knows are just as virile as your generation of students."

"Some of them certainly don't look it, any more than she looks feminine. I never could stand these 'anything you can do, I can do better' females."

As he finished speaking, the telephone in the hall began to ring. Jane heard Mary say, "Oh, bother! Who can that be?" and go quickly downstairs to find out. At the same time David disappeared into the bathroom further along the landing. She heard the click of the slide-lock and, a few seconds later, the sound of both taps running at full pressure. Seizing her opportunity, she sped across the landing and down the right-angled passage which led to her bedroom.

It was a long time since she had cried, but there were tears in her eyes when she closed the door. Suddenly, while she was being forced to listen to David's opinion of her, the realisation of what a long, lonely road she had chosen to follow had gripped her with an almost physical chill.

It was not the first time she had felt discouraged. Occasional fits of depression were part of any prolonged and taxing endeavour. But it was the first time she had actually heard herself described as "frumpish" and "heavy going" and, foolishly no doubt, she could not help feeling both hurt and humiliated.

In justice to David Carleton, she had to admit that she had not tried to disguise the antagonism he aroused in her. But she would not have felt it if *his* attitude had been the impersonal friendliness with which his brother-in-law treated her.

I was so happy here – until he arrived, she thought desolately. Indeed it was only now, after he had disrupted it, that she recognised the first part of her stay with the Wroxhams as

36

the most contented and secure period of her life since very early childhood.

If life had taught Jane anything, it was that if something unpleasant or difficult had to be done, it was best to tackle it immediately.

So the following morning, before breakfast, she said to Mary Wroxham, "Do you think, in the circumstances, it would be better if I didn't come abroad with you? I'm sure I can get another job for the rest of the vacation. You needn't feel you have to keep me on now that poor Doctor Swanton's collapse has changed everything."

"Not keep you on?" Mrs. Wroxham echoed, looking astonished. "Whatever put that idea in your head, Jane? Why should I want you to leave us?"

"Well, your brother and I don't seem to get on very well, and I thought perhaps —"

"This isn't a roundabout way of saying that *you* don't want to come with us, is it?" Mary interrupted.

"Oh, no — not at all. I've been looking forward to it. But —"

"As far as I'm concerned, you're a most necessary member of the party," Mary assured her. "I should have a very flat time of it, alone with David. He would go off in pursuit of some glamorous girl, and I should be left to spend the evening alone. As it is, we'll make him do his share of the baby-sitting, and you and I will have a few evenings out."

"If you're sure . . ."

"Quite sure, my dear," Mary said firmly.

As passengers on the Norfolk Line ferry were required to arrive at the dock at four in the morning, it was necessary for the camping party to set out from home at three a.m. On Tuesday evening the children were given a mild sedative and, except John, were put to bed in the van.

"With luck, they'll sleep all the way to the docks," said their mother.

On Doctor Wroxham's advice, Jane also had a pill. It was so effective that she was woken, not by her little alarm clock, but by someone rocking her shoulder. She opened her eyes to find David and John looking down at her.

"Come on, Jane. It's time to go," John announced excitedly.

CHAPTER II

JANE was not properly in bed, but had been sleeping, dressed, between blankets. It did not take long to clean her teeth, comb her hair, and put on her shoes and outdoor garments. But it was some time before she felt completely clear-headed, and by then the belt of golden lights which marked the outer ring road surrounding the city was in sight.

"Doesn't Norwich seem queer without any people bustling about?" remarked John, peering over Jane's shoulder, as they passed through the brightly lit but deserted shopping centre.

At Thorpe, on the eastern fringe of the city, the River Yare was lined with holidaymakers' cabin cruisers, the portholes curtained, the passengers sleeping. Soon they were in the darkness of the countryside once more, an endless ribbon of cat's eyes gleaming in the beam of the headlamps.

"I think Mummy is asleep," whispered John.

Certainly Mary's eyes were closed, but perhaps, not because she was dozing, but to hide her unhappiness at leaving her husband behind.

It must be wonderful to have a marriage like the Wroxhams', thought Jane. But it was so rare; and the other kind of marriage, such as her parents had endured, was so intolerable. It was frightening to realise that within a short time of imagining that they wanted to spend their whole lives together, a couple could reach the point when it was difficult to get through one day without having a row. Even now her mind flinched from the memory of the quarrels which had punctuated her childhood. Neither of her parents had been willing to admit that they were partly responsible for the failure of the marriage. Her mother had considered that it was entirely her

39

father's fault, while he had laid the blame on her mother. Yet from an early age Jane, the onlooker, had seen that it was not her mother's nagging, or her father's bursts of savage temper, which had wrecked their relationship. These were only the side effects of a basic incompatibility. With other partners, the worst sides of her parents' natures might have remained dormant. But, dazzled by a transient attraction, they had failed to see that, in every way, they could scarcely have been less suited.

Not wishing to pursue a train of thought which conjured so many unpleasant recollections, she glanced at David. Perhaps he had not had a pill, like the rest of them, or perhaps he was more accustomed to starting journeys at strange hours. His face was close-shaven, his grey eyes alert. So alert that he sensed her glance and returned it.

"Did you forget to set your clock?"

"No, the sleeping tablet knocked me out. I've never had one before."

He lifted an eyebrow. "That's unusual in this day and age."

She remembered his jibe about present-day male students, and was tempted to point out that, whatever he might suppose, there were many undergraduates who did not take pep pills, tranquillizers or any other kind of pill. But she kept silent, for if he was one of those people who regarded all students as long-haired anarchists, it was unlikely that she could change his opinion.

On the outskirts of Great Yarmouth, Mary told her brother which roads to take to reach the wharf, lit by powerful arc lamps, where the *Duke of Holland* was being loaded.

They were welcomed on board by the Purser, a friendly young Dutchman who spoke fluent, idiomatic English, and who remembered Mary and the children from the summer before.

In spite of the narrowness and steepness of the stairs up to the passenger-cabin deck, and the noise made by the cargo containers as they rumbled across the ramp, David was able to transfer the two youngest children from the van to their bunks without waking them. Thomas was sharing a cabin with his mother. The twins were together. Jane was to share with Francesca, and David with John.

Although they had woken up, the twins were put to bed with instructions to try to sleep, at least until breakfast time. Only John was allowed to accompany the adults to the saloon on the next deck up, to have coffee, and to watch the extraordinary ease and rapidity with which the powerful shiploaders manoeuvred the thirty-foot-long containers with their distinctive bright blue tarpaulins. The most fascinating thing about the ship-loaders was that the drivers could slide their steering compartments from side to side by means of a device much like the carriage on a typewriter.

"I think that's what I'll be when I grow up. A ship-loader driver," said John admiringly.

Mary drained her cup of coffee. "I'm going to bed. Coming, Jane?"

At five o'clock, after lying in her upper berth for nearly an hour, too excited now even to doze, Jane climbed down the ladder and put on her shoes. Francesca was soundly asleep, and looked as if she would not wake for a couple of hours.

In the passage outside the cabin, Jane met John. "Shall I show you round?" he offered.

"Yes, all right. Where's your uncle? In bed?"

"No, he's somewhere around."

John ended his guided tour on the smallest, topmost deck where, in fine weather, passengers could enjoy the North Sea breezes. It was growing light, and the dawn wind carried the smell of timber, and oil, and the open sea. The tide was on the turn, and the surface of the river was rippled and swirled by strong undercurrents.

"No, I think I'll be a captain," murmured John, and presently she saw he was absorbed in a small boy's daydream; that now, in his mind, he was Captain Wroxham, hero of countless stirring exploits.

41

Leaning on the rail of a ship seemed to be conducive to day-dreaming. Before long Jane's own imagination was at work, transporting her from the present to a future in which, beautifully dressed, completely self-assured, she was standing on the deck of a liner bound for a three-week cruise in the Mediterranean.

"Here comes the pilot's launch."

With a start of surprise she returned to reality, and found that John was no longer beside her. His place had been taken by David.

She glanced at her watch, and was amazed to discover how long she had been lost in thought. "I'd better go down to the cabin. Francesca may have woken up," she said.

David made no remark, but he was watching her with an expression which reminded her what he had said about her on Monday night. *"She can't relax if there's a man around."*

Her cheeks grew hot. Let him think what he liked about her!

Soon, the *Duke of Holland* was moving slowly down river. In the saloon, some of the ship's officers, and the four truck drivers who made up the twelve passengers the ferry could carry, were having a substantial Dutch breakfast of cooked meats, thin slices of Edam cheese, and bread and butter with jam.

By the time Mary Wroxham's party had finished breakfast, the ferry was on the open sea, and the pilot's launch was on its way back to the mouth of the harbour. Soon the flat coastline of Norfolk had disappeared. There was nothing to be seen through the wide, stern-facing window, but the sunlit sea, and half a dozen hopeful gulls gliding above the ship's wake.

"Here's to a happy trip," said Mary, raising her coffee cup. "I wonder where we shall sleep tonight?"

They spent their first night abroad at Strandhaus Sonsfeld, a camp about twenty miles inside the German frontier. Mary had selected the place from her camping guide because it was not much of a detour from their route south, yet was not too close

42

to the *autobahn* or any large town.

They entered the camp through a farmyard and, when they arrived at about half past five in the evening, the site seemed almost full up. But a woman at the camp shop told them that they could pitch on a space close to the farmhouse, under a large tree.

"Can we go for a swim, Mum?" asked John. As the guide book had indicated, the camp was on the edge of a lake, and the water looked very inviting after the hot, ninety-mile drive from the Dutch port of Scheveningen.

"Not until you've helped to put up the tent," said his mother firmly. "Then we'll all bathe."

Until she had taken her holiday job with the Wroxhams, Jane had always thought of camping in terms of small, cramped ridge tents into which people had to crawl on their hands and knees or, at best, bent double. But soon after she joined the household, the Wroxhams had practised pitching their newly acquired French frame tent in the back garden. With three adults and the three eldest children all lending a hand, it had taken them less than half an hour to put up the whole thing, including the insect-proof yellow bedroom compartments, the zipp-on kitchen extension, and the porch and window canopies. Inside, there was ample headroom, even for a man of David's height.

This time, as Sonsfeld was only an overnight stop, they did not bother with the extension or the scallop-edged canopies.

"We'll deal with the bedding when we've cooled off in the lake," said Mary presently. There was no breeze, and the atmosphere was very close, suggesting a storm to come. "Here are your bathing things, children. You can take first turn in the van, Jane. I'm going to buy a bottle of wine for our supper. Would you rather have wine or beer, David?"

Jane retired into the van and drew the checked gingham curtains. She had scarcely undressed before the children were thumping on the door.

"Hurry up, Jane!"

"You go on. I shan't be long," she called.

Both her bathing suits had originally belonged to Bettina who bought several every summer and discarded them almost brand new by Jane's standards. Had she been buying a swimsuit, she would have chosen something more conservative than the eye-catching, maximum-exposure styles favoured by her friend. But although she had scruples about inheriting too many things from Bettina, it did seem foolish to spend precious book-money on swimsuits when her friend had so many cast-offs which, if Jane did not rescue them, would find their way to the dustbin.

Thus it was that when she emerged from the van, she was wearing a pale blue bikini of a brevity made doubly arresting by the fact that her figure and legs were usually concealed by jeans, baggy sweaters and shapeless shirts.

Several long days on the Norfolk coast with Mary and the children had already given her a light tan, and most girls of her age would have been gratified by the knowledge that they possessed precisely the kind of rounded slenderness for which bikinis were designed. But when Jane stepped down from the van just as David strolled back from the shop with a bottle of beer, her chief feeling was one of mortification because he would not know that the frivolous suit was not of her choosing.

"You look ten degrees cooler already," he said, and the way he looked at her made her feel like a girl in a slave market.

Flushing, she hastened past him to join the children.

It was evident that most of the caravans on the grassy slope between the farm buildings and the lakeside were parked there for the season. They were surrounded by neat, low-fenced gardens, and many of them had canvas extensions. On the other side of the lake, black and white cows were browsing on a peaceful expanse of flat pastureland.

An area of shallow water had been railed off, and the twins and Francesca were already splashing about in this section. Thomas was crouched near a see-saw, examining something at his feet.

44

"Come and look at my snake, Jane."

She went to admire the earthworm. Thomas loved worms and spent hours of his life murmuring to them. She had once seen him tenderly stroking one.

"Come on, Jane. Let's swim to the other side." John was waiting for her on a narrow jetty-cum-diving-board.

Although Mary's guide described the camp's swimming place as a lake, it looked more like a quiet stretch of river about fifty yards wide. Perhaps it was an ox-bow lake, thought Jane, as she followed John off the end of the jetty.

She was with him, treading water midway between the banks, when she noticed Mary Wroxham and her brother walking down the slope. Mary was in a navy stretch-terry two-piece of the kind Jane would have preferred. She did not register the colour of David's shorts because the most noticeable things about him were his head-to-heel South American tan, and his look of fitness. The breadth of his shoulders was apparent when he was fully dressed. But in the short time since his arrival there had been nothing overtly athletic in his bearing, nothing to suggest that his clothes and his rather indolent carriage concealed the powerful physique of a man who, though he might relax when on leave, obviously kept himself in excellent shape between furloughs.

"What's it like in?" called Mary.

"Lovely!" Jane answered. She turned on her back and floated, annoyed by the realisation that it was unreasonable to resent David's appraisal of her figure, and then to look at him in much the same way.

"Uncle David is a fantastic diver and underwater swimmer," said John. "Look, he's coming in now."

Politeness obliged Jane to right herself, but David had already disappeared when she looked towards the jetty.

"Goodness knows where he'll come up," said his nephew admiringly. "He can hold his breath for *ages*."

I hope he isn't one of those idiots who think it's amusing to grab people's feet, thought Jane. Although she loved the

45

water, she hated the sensation of being pulled under, even in fun. As the seconds passed and the surface of the lake remained unbroken, she braced herself for the sudden tug, the horrid feeling of being caught, unable even to struggle.

Her alarm was unnecessary. David surfaced several yards away.

"Mm ... that feels better," he said, smiling at John. "How about a race to the rails?"

"Okay. Ready ... steady ... *go*!" Arms flailing, the boy shot off

Reluctantly, Jane had to admire the two or three strong, easy strokes with which his uncle overhauled him.

When Mary said it was time to come out, and they returned to the tent, the camp shop was selling chips. David and John went to buy some while Jane and Mary supervised the drying and dressing of the younger children. Then they all sat down to enjoy the hot chips which were served in paper comes with little wooden forks so that people could keep their fingers clean.

Presently, while Mary was cooking bacon and eggs in two large frying pans on the butane gas cooker, David inflated the two double airbeds, and the single one which the Wroxhams had bought for Jane's use but which, now, he was to sleep on.

By half past eight, all the children were snugly cocooned in their sleeping bags, and even John was too tired to beg for some reading time.

"How about a short walk before we turn in?" suggested Mary. "Oddly enough, considering how little sleep we had last night, I don't feel particularly tired now."

Strolling along the country road outside the camping ground, they discovered that the main entrance was some distance from their way in through the farmyard. Indeed the ground was a much larger one than they had realised, and its facilities included a restaurant with a terrace overlooking the river, a discotheque for the younger campers, and a coin-operated mini merry-go-round which would have delighted the Wroxham children had they known of it.

There were very few people in the restaurant, but the windows of the discotheque showed that several couples were dancing, and other young people were sitting about, talking.

"Wouldn't you like to go in, Jane?" Mary suggested. "You haven't had a night out since you came to us."

"Oh, no, thank you," Jane said hastily.

"Don't you care for dancing?" David asked her.

"Sometimes," she said off-handedly. But the truth was that although most of the people in the discotheque were young men and girls of about her age, and probably several of them were students, she had neither the inclination or the assurance to go inside and make friends.

"Could it be that there are some circumstances in which even feminists prefer to be under a masculine wing?" he murmured sardonically.

Jane pretended not to hear this remark and, to her relief, Mary stopped watching the scene through the windows, and said, "Such energy! It makes me feel tired just to watch. Still, I don't suppose those young things got up quite as early as we did."

During the night there was a storm which woke Jane, and rather alarmed her. Normally she did not mind thunder or lightning, but on this occasion she could not help thinking of what would happen to the tent if the tree above it should be struck. It was a relief when the storm passed over. For a while she lay listening to the rain, and thinking how lucky she was to have landed this job – if helping with five such nice, biddable children could be called a job. Then, too, it was luxury to her to have three good meals every day. Like a number of undergraduates with so-called 'middle class' backgrounds, Jane was considerably worse off than students whose parents were in a lower income group. They received the full Government grant during their years at university. Because Richard Kirstead was well off, Jane received only a partial grant which, after she had paid the rent for her bedsitter, did not stretch to the kind of food provided by Mrs. Wroxham.

Several times during their friendship, Bettina Brooke had urged Jane to give up the somewhat dreary bedsitter, and come to share her pleasant flat. If, instead of contributing to the rent, Jane kept the place in order and did the shopping, they would both be better off, she had said persuasively. It had been a tempting proposition because it was true that Bettina was hopelessly disorganised in all matters domestic, and the flat would have been much more tidy and comfortable had Jane had the running of it.

However, after much thought, Jane had decided to stay where she was; not because the arrangement suggested by her friend would have been inequitable, or fretted her pride, but because at the bed-sitter she might often be hungry and, in winter, cold as well, but at least she could concentrate on her studies in a way that would be impossible at the flat. Bettina was a nocturnal being who could sit up till all hours, and whose brain was as efficient at two a.m. as at two p.m. Jane had a diurnal temperament. Without nine hours' sleep – preferably three before midnight – she became heavy-eyed and dull-witted.

But perhaps that is partly a diet deficiency, because I didn't feel washed out yesterday, she reflected.

The rain had ceased now, although the branches of the tree were still dripping gently. She was about to turn over and go back to sleep when she thought she heard voices. She raised herself and parted the curtains.

A light, showing the way to the washrooms, was left on all night. But there seemed to be no one about. Perhaps she had imagined the voices. Then, as she was about to let the curtain fall back into place, someone flashed a torchlight inside the tent. Was it David? Or one of the children, trying to wake him? Supposing one of them was ill? Supposing he was a heavy sleeper, or did not take kindly to being disturbed when they did manage to rouse him? Ought she to go and find out what was wrong, or to wake Mary?

Before she had made up her mind, the tent flap was unzipped and David emerged, followed by his younger niece. Unaware of being watched from the van, they set off, hand in hand, for the washroom block. Francesca looked tiny beside her uncle. She had on her scarlet Wellingtons and, in place of a dressing-gown, David's navy sweater, worn like a cloak.

Goodness, that's rash of him. She'll probably forget to bunch it up, and it will get soaked, thought Jane, with a rather malicious grin. Yet, as she watched the little girl disappearing into one of the loos, and the tall man waiting for her outside, his hands in the pockets of his mac, his shoulders slightly hunched against the chill after the storm, her amusement was mixed with another feeling, one not easy to analyse.

She did not want him to catch sight of her face at the window, as he was sure to do on the way back, so she let the curtain fall, and lay down.

"I always imagined that people who went in for camping holidays would be up at dawn, doing physical jerks," said Jane, at breakfast next morning.

It was half past seven, and she and Mary had been up for an hour. But the surrounding caravans still had their curtains closed, and so far very few people had passed by on their way to the washrooms.

"No, considering how early most campers turn in at night, they're surprisingly late risers," said Mary. "Have you noticed that the majority of Continental campers live in stretch-nylon track suits? I think I might buy some for the children, if they're not too expensive."

"Did you bring any needles and thread, Mary?" asked David, after he had finished his second cup of black coffee.

"Yes, indeed – most essential!" she answered. "Have you lost a button?"

"No, I notice that one of the tent zipps is coming adrift. I'll fix it before it gets worse."

To Jane, whose father, stepfather and stepbrothers would all have regarded such a task as women's work, the sight of

49

David choosing, from the contents of his sister's work basket, a strong needle and a reel of button thread was as unexpected as if Mary had suddenly lit up a pipe of tobacco.

Unlike many camping vans, the Wroxhams' van did not have a built-in sink. Except in a downpour, washing up was done outside the van. As Jane tied on a navy blue butcher's apron, preparatory to doing the breakfast dishes, she could not help watching the surprising competence with which David was mending the loose zipper.

"You've forgotten to put on gloves again, you bad girl," Mary scolded presently, when she emerged after tidying the van and found Jane scouring a saucepan with unprotected hands.

"I feel all thumbs in gloves."

"So does everyone, at first. But one soon gets used to them; and you'll ruin your hands if you don't make a habit of wearing them."

"I haven't got pretty hands anyway," said Jane, as she dried them. Mary's hands were elegantly narrow, deserving the care she gave them. But Jane's were square, like a boy's hands.

"Oh, I wouldn't say that," remarked David, ducking out of the tent.

She thought he had gone to give Thomas a ride on the see-saw, and was startled by his sudden appearance, and even more startled when he took one of her hands in his and, snapping his heels together, bowed over it. But instead of kissing her fingers, he sniffed them.

"Hm, yes . . . dishwater," he pronounced wryly. "I prefer the scent of handcream. You'd better take Mary's advice, or you could become the sad case of the girl who came to Europe and never had her hand kissed."

Jane snatched her fingers away. "I wasn't expecting to have it kissed."

His grey eyes glinted. "But hoping, no doubt? Surely even a feminist is not averse to a spot of Continental gallantry?" Before she could reply, he added briskly, "If you two have finished your chores, we'd better start getting the tent down."

Soon after they set out that morning, it began to rain, and David suggested that, instead of travelling south by easy stages, it might be a better idea to make one long haul while the weather was poor.

"Exactly how far are we from the Black Forest area?" he asked his sister, who was sitting in front to navigate while Jane kept an eye on the children in the back of the van.

Mary consulted her maps. "I make it two hundred and eighty miles from here to Baden-Baden which is where the Hochstrasse – the Forest High Road – begins," she said doubtfully. "That's far too long a day's run for the children, David."

"I expect Jane can keep them amused."

"For over five hours? Poor Jane!"

"Well, let's see how it goes, shall we?" said David.

With several short coffee-stops, and a longer break for lunch, they travelled more than three hundred miles that day. It was half-past five when at last they reached their final stopping place, a camp site several kilometres from Freudenstadt, a town deep in the Schwarzwald. By then Jane was very glad to climb down from the van for the last time.

The camp was at the top of a hill, and they pitched the tent close to the edge of the sloping cornfield which gave them an uninterrupted view across a wide valley.

The rain-clouds had cleared, and they ate their supper in the open air, watching a sunset which more than made up for the rather wearisome day whirling along the *autobahn*. The hollows of the hills were already filling with mist as the sun sank behind the forested heights on the far side of the valley. Slowly, the sky changed from sulphur to flame and then to hot pink and orange. Finally the brilliant colours faded into a pearly rose tone which in turn became faintest lavender.

Looking toy-sized from the height of their vantage point, a steam train chugged across a viaduct, leaving a plume of white smoke. The distant lights of Freudenstadt illumined the deepening darkness. Somewhere, a farm dog barked.

"Ah, this is peaceful," murmured Mary. "Smell that fresh air! Lovely!"

"More coffee, Jane?" asked David, leaning towards her with pot outstretched.

"Oh . . . no, thanks," she said, rather abstractedly. Suddenly, watching the sun go down, she had become intensely aware of how beautiful the world was, and how little of it she had seen.

There was a small bar-shop at the entrance to the camp and, after the children were in bed, the grown-ups went for a drink.

"I hadn't realised it would be dark so early here," said Mary, as her brother shone a torch along the grass for them. "Perhaps we should have come for the first three weeks of the school holidays. But then the last weeks would have been such an anti-climax."

There was no one in the bar but the warden of the camp, a handsome old man with thick white hair and a good command of English. When he had poured out glasses of wine for the women, and beer for David, he turned on a television set, thinking no doubt that, in the absence of any fellow campers, it would provide some entertainment for them. But Mary had brought her writing case with her, and started a letter to her husband; and, presently, his beer finished, David said, "After driving all day I need some exercise. Would you care to come along, Jane?"

She would have liked a stroll – with anyone else! Besides, she knew he was only being polite, and would much rather go on his own.

"I don't think so, thank you."

Mary glanced up from her letter. "Don't mind me. I shall be busy for some time. Do go if you want to, Jane."

Afterwards, Jane thought it must have been the wine which made her change her mind, and say, "Very well. I could do with a short walk."

"Let's have a look at that tower down by the copse, shall we?" said David, outside the bar. It was no longer necessary for him to shine the torch. Some clouds which had hidden the moon a short time earlier had blown away, and the camp and surrounding countryside were bathed in silvery light.

They followed the path, crossed by power lines and flanked at intervals by small rubbish bins, which led across the camp to an adjoining meadow. Beyond the fence, the path narrowed, leading to a small wood. The tower which was their objective was a squat edifice with an external stairway winding upwards. They climbed to the top where they found what looked at first glance like a sundial, but was actually a large metal disc inscribed with the names, directions and heights of various peaks which, presumably, could be seen from the tower in clear weather.

For a minute or two they both bent over the disc, trying to make out all the names, which was not easy by moonlight. Then, more interested in the view, Jane moved away to rest her elbows on the outer wall of the tower, and gaze about her.

"What's the matter?" asked David, misunderstanding her movement. "Has it occurred to you that although you're my intellectual equal, your brain-power won't be much help if I choose to kiss you?"

Jane felt her cheeks burn and wondered if, in that light, the colour showed. "I don't think I need to worry about that contingency," she said, in her coolest tone.

"No? What makes you so sure?" As he spoke, he came to lean on the parapet, about a yard away from her.

She controlled her instinct to put a greater distance between them. "I credit you with some discrimination. I'm not the kind of girl who would attract you."

"Really? What kind of girls do attract me, do you suppose?"

She noticed his use of the plural. It seemed to confirm her supposition that he thought of women collectively, never of finding one girl with whom to establish a lasting relationship.

"Decorative ones." She had meant to leave it at that, but found herself elaborating. "Pretty, fashionable girls who will attract attention when you take them about. Girls who listen, and agree, and never, ever argue with you."

"Soft, sweet, sexy dumb blondes – although the colour of their hair isn't important providing they have all the other qualifications. Does that sum them up?" he asked lightly.

"Perfectly, I should imagine."

He laughed. "You're an odd girl. Usually, when egghead females are withering about pretty featherbrains, one suspects sour grapes. But that obviously isn't the reason in your case. I'm beginning to think you're a split personality. No true feminist ever bought herself a bathing suit like that blue thing you were wearing last night. Your *alter ego* must have been in control the day you went shopping for that."

"It was given to me," Jane informed him.

"By someone who knows you better than you do yourself, I should guess."

"By a girl friend who looks like one of your favourite dumb blonde types, but who is actually very intelligent. I only wish you could meet her. Belinda would really shake up your ideas about women."

"You seem very sure that you know what I think about women."

"I think you agree with the person who said – 'I believe in the natural superiority of man as I believe in the existence of God.' "

He said dryly, "Now *you* are guilty of being superior, my girl."

"What do you mean?"

"I'm sure you know who made that statement. But you take it for granted that I won't. It was made by one of your own sex, Caroline Norton, an early Victorian authoress – correct?"

"Yes," she admitted.

He straightened. "It's been a long day. We'd better go back and get some sleep."

As they were descending the stone staircase, she said, "Yes, it was unfair. I apologize."

At the foot of the steps, he stopped and turned, his expression inscrutable in the shadow of the tower wall. "On that note, would it be a good idea – since we've been thrown together, as they say – to try to forget the battle of the sexes for the duration of the trip?"

"We can try," she agreed uncertainly.

"It shouldn't be too hard, for three weeks." As easily as if she were Emma's size, he took her by the waist and swung her to the ground.

The valley was shrouded in mist and there was a heavy dew greying the grass when, soon after six the next morning, Jane went to the washroom. Although all the caravans had been curtained as she passed them, and all the tent flaps closed, she was not the only early riser. Someone was whistling cheerfully in the men's washroom.

There was no hot water, and she could not steel herself to have a cold shower. Even to wash thoroughly at one of the basins called for considerable resolution. She had felt chilly during the night, and she was shivering as she washed her neck and ears. By the time she reached her feet, her teeth were chattering.

With its concrete floor and central drain, the washroom was a dreary place. She was glad to leave it. As she did so, David came out of the opposite door.

"Good lord! You look blue," he exclaimed, as soon as he saw her.

"I feel it," she admitted.

He took her free hand in his, and gave a wordless exclamation at the iciness of her skin. His own was warm, and as comforting as a lined glove against her chilled fingers.

"Hot coffee is what you need, my girl." Keeping hold of her hand, he hurried her back to the tent, his long strides forcing Jane to break into a trot to keep pace with him.

She did not have to wait for the water to boil. There had been some hot water to spare the night before, and he had poured it into a vacuum flask.

"What a good idea. I wouldn't have thought of that," she

said, watching him stir spoonfuls of powdered milk into two mugs of instant coffee.

"I've just had a better idea." David ducked inside the tent where the children were beginning to stir, and came out with the sturdy canvas grip which was all his luggage. From the central compartment, safely bedded among his clothes, he extracted an unopened bottle of whisky. "Duty-free Scotch from the Purser on board the ferry," he explained. "Will you take it neat, or in your coffee?"

"Please don't open the bottle on my account –" she began.

He ignored this, and poured a small measure into a plastic egg-cup.

"I'm not used to alcohol. It will make me tight," she protested, as he offered it to her.

"That thimbleful? Nonsense. Drink it!" he ordered. "Unless you'd prefer to be held tight?"

"W-what?"

"If there's no other way of doing it, one can warm a severely chilled person by holding them close. Didn't you know that?"

"That's only in cases of exposure." She swallowed the whisky in one gulp, as if it were medicine, and shuddered.

He grinned. "I thought that would make you drink it! 'Morning, John. Sleep well?" – as his eldest nephew emerged from the tent.

At breakfast, it was decided to spend the morning exploring Freudenstadt. Their first stop was at the Grossmarkt, a supermarket on the outskirts of the town. It was here that the children discovered that for one mark they could buy a big bag of crisp salt sticks which were not only delicious to nibble but, used in place of matches, added zest to games of rummy and dice.

After Mary had replenished her stock of perishable food, they drove on to the centre of Freudenstadt, a vast park-like square surrounded on all four sides by a shopping arcade. Not only were the shop windows full of dolls in the traditional

56

costumes of the region, but a great many of the tourists, middle-aged women as well as girls, were wearing the pinafore-style folk dresses known as *dirndls*. And everywhere there were tourists whose buckled breeches, stout boots, and spike-tipped sticks indicated that they were on a rambling holiday.

Although it did not rain that day, the sky remained overcast and their picnic lunch along a lane leading deep into the pine forests was not as pleasant as it would have been in bright sunshine.

But next morning, when they had already decided to press on south to the Swiss frontier, the sun broke through the early mist, and was still shining when, late in the afternoon, they came to the top of a hill and saw below them the pewter-grey gleam of the Rhine, and the small border town of Waldshut.

The camping site was on the bank of the river, in a willow grove, with the towpath affording a pleasant short cut into town. It was evident, both from the muddiness of the path, and the speed with which the river was flowing, that there had been heavy and prolonged rain in the area. But fortunately there was a recently vacated and consequently dry space for their tent between a small British caravan and a large Swiss one.

It was when they had finished pitching the tent that Jane discovered the loss of her shabby soft-top suitcase. At first it seemed that it must be somewhere among the baggage. But it was not. Jane searched: Mary searched: they all searched. It could not be found.

"Where can it have gone? What am I to do?" she exclaimed, in bewildered consternation. The case contained everything but the clothes she was wearing, and which she had intended to wash before supper.

"Don't look so shattered. It's a nuisance, but not a disaster," David said calmingly.

"There was nothing valuable in the case, was there?" asked Mary, her tone more concerned. "No jewellery, or anything like that?"

"No, I don't possess any jewellery. But my clothes were valuable – to me," Jane added defensively, thinking she saw a sardonic glint in David's eyes.

"But not irreplaceable." He glanced at his watch. "The shops in town will be closed now, but a place of this size should be able to provide all you need tomorrow. You can hold out until the morning, can't you?"

"Tomorrow is Sunday," his sister reminded him. "Never mind, Jane. You can borrow some of my kit for the week-end, and first thing on Monday we'll go shopping."

After supper, when the children were in bed, Mary proposed a visit to the camp café which seemed to enjoy more custom than the rather dismal little bar-shop at the previous camp. "You'll be going into town, I suppose, as it's not far to walk?" she remarked to her brother.

"I shouldn't think there's very much night life in Waldshut. I'll come to the café with you two," he said.

Jane was still upset by the loss of her case. She was certain that she had stowed it in its usual place in the van before they set out that morning. There could be no question of it having been left behind at the last camp. It was conceivable that objects such as tent pegs, combs and odd coins might be missed in the final check; but a suitcase, even a small one, could not possibly be overlooked. The only solution to the mystery seemed to be that David had forgotten to lock the van when they had stopped to see the waterfall at Triberg, and that during their absence someone had stolen the case.

It seemed a curious thing to steal, but perhaps, in the absence of any quickly-snatched valuables such as radios and cameras, a thief would grab the first piece of portable loot in sight, and hope for the best.

She did not ask David if he could remember locking the van, but he must have guessed the direction of her thoughts as he said, "Still worrying about your lost clothes?"

She said, as cheerfully as she could, "Not *worrying*, but I can't help wondering about them."

At this, perhaps with the object of giving Jane something else to think about, Mary suggested they should emulate the Swiss campers on the other side of the room who were having a lively game of cards.

"I have the pack in my bag," she added, unzipping the shoulder bag which she had bought specially for the trip, so that wherever they went she could carry travellers' cheques, passports and motoring documents without the encumbrance of an ordinary bag.

Mary dealt the cards first, followed rather inexpertly by Jane. Then it was David's turn and, watching him deftly shuffle the pack without dropping cards as she had done, Jane suddenly found herself wondering what it would be like to be caressed by those strong brown hands which, in spite of their unmistakable masculinity, could ply a needle and thread every stitch as neatly as her own fingers.

It was such an extraordinary thing to catch herself thinking that, as she picked up the cards he had dealt her, her cheeks burned with colour. Then, to add to her embarrassment, David spoke to her.

"Is that boy in the corner annoying you? Shall I deal with him?"

The question bewildered her. Until that moment she had not noticed that there was a young man in the corner of the café directly opposite her seat. He was by himself, his elbows on the edge of the table, his shoulders hunched, his chin propped upon the heel of one half-clenched hand. He appeared to have been watching the three English card-players, but as Jane looked at him, he averted his gaze.

"How could he be annoying me? I hadn't even noticed him," she said, in genuine puzzlement.

"No?" David looked amused and sceptical. "Then why the maidenly blush?"

Her colour deepened. "If I'm flushed it must be because it's rather close in here," she answered, her eyes fixed on the cards in her hand.

"He looks rather a nice lad," said Mary. "Oh, he's gulped down his beer, and he's leaving. You've put him off by glowering at him, David."

"Why should I glower at him?" said her brother. "I'm not Jane's keeper. I merely offered to deal with him if she found his scrutiny embarrassing – which, judging by her blushes, she did."

"He looked lonely. Perhaps he would have liked to join us," remarked Mary.

"How about it, Jane? Would you like to meet your admirer? Shall I go after him and invite him to make a fourth?" David enquired.

Jane had recovered her self-possession. "He probably doesn't speak English," she answered, more calmly, and he did not tease her any more.

Next morning she was woken at seven by the clangour of church bells. Mary and Thomas slept on, undisturbed by the sound. Presently, raising herself on one elbow, Jane drew back the curtain from the window close beside her pillow, and watched the wide waters of the Rhine surging eastwards only a few yards from where she lay. Within her range of vision there was a notice warning campers that the river was not safe for bathing. Watching the constantly changing pattern of eddies, Jane thought that, if she fell in, her only hope would be to keep afloat and pray that eventually the current would carry her across to the far bank. She doubted if even as powerful a swimmer as David could cross the river without being swept far downstream.

After a late breakfast, they drove to Schaffhausen to see the Rheinfall. It was a bright, hot morning and, in addition to scores of foreign holidaymakers, many Sunday-best-dressed local people were passing up and down the stairways and along the footpaths surrounding the seventy-foot torrent of roaring, sparkling white foam, the most powerful waterfall in Europe.

John and the twins were eager to go on one of the boats taking parties of tourists to the great rock, half way across the falls. But Mary would not yield to their pleas because, although the rock was obviously a wonderful vantage point, it was equally obvious that the people on it, unless they had plastic raincoats, were all drenched by the mist-thick veils of spray surrounding the crag.

"Your mother is right. It would be stupid to get wet deliberately," said David, when they appealed to him for support!

He sounded rather impatient and bored, Jane thought.

The children soon forgot their disappointment in their interest in the large chubb cruising in the still golden depths of a backwater at the end of the wide promenade where the river regained its calm after the wild turbulence of the falls. But all at once the water lost its golden transparency, and they realised the sun had gone in.

"Oh, dear! Look how black the sky is," Mary exclaimed. "There's going to be a deluge before long. I think we should start walking back to the car-park."

They had gone only a short distance before the first large, slow drops of rain began to splash down. There was barely time to reach the shelter provided by the canopy of one of the promenade cafés before the downpour began, rapidly soaking everyone not under cover.

"It may not last long," said Mary hopefully, as they stood looking out at the Rheinfall, now directly in front of them.

Half an hour later, when the rain was still bucketing down, David said dryly, "Whatever else we forget out of this trip, the Rheinfall will be an indelible memory."

But when Jane glanced at him again, a few minutes later, he was no longer watching the ceaseless white torrent of the falls. Instead he was looking at a very pretty German tourist who was coming through the turnstile of the *Damen*, near where Mrs. Wroxham and her party were standing.

The girl seemed to be on her own. She was wearing a particularly attractive folk dress of brown material with bands of black velvet sewn round the lower part of the full skirt. Her white blouse, under the low-cut bodice of the *dirndl*, was trimmed with lace and beautifully laundered. Her hair, make-up and shoes were in the current fashion, and she looked no less modern than the trousered and mini-dressed girls of other nationalities in the cosmopolitan crowd taking shelter. Yet somehow the tight-waisted folk costume gave her something which the others lacked; an air of extreme femininity which reminded Jane of Harriet Martham in her red midi skirt.

It was not long before the girl noticed David. Jane, in her place, would have tried to ignore his appreciative gaze.

The girl in the *dirndl* returned his regard with an unmistakable twinkle in her eyes. Clearly she did not object to being admired by a personable stranger (whom she probably guessed to be a foreigner), and saw no reason to hide the fact that she liked the look of him.

At this point Jane was distracted by a remark from Mary, and by the time her attention was free once more, David and the girl were in conversation. Watching them, Jane felt a pang of something which, unwillingly, she recognised as envy. What is happening to me? she thought, alarmed. It shocked her that, even for a moment, her carefully-planned future could seem less important than her urgent desire to outshine the other girl *now*.

That night, when Mary again suggested going to the camp café for an hour, Jane thought it tactful to pretend to want an early night. But after the others had gone, and she had been to the washroom, she put her towel and her toilet bag – which, fortunately, had not been in her suitcase at the time of its disappearance – in the van, and then crossed the few yards to the towpath to watch the river for a while.

She had been there, thinking, for some time, when a voice behind her said, "Good evening." Turning, she saw the fair-haired young man who, according to David, had been staring at her in the café the night before.

"You have had an enjoyable day?" he enquired.

mustard cardigan which Jane had bought in a sale because
as cheap. But it was no use. Mary was determined to make
look more presentable and, after a few more lame objec-
s, Jane's resistance crumpled, and she allowed herself to
verruled.

t was while the saleswoman was folding everything that
ry noticed the dress.

"Oh, Jane, do look at this! Isn't it charming?" She took
m a rail a dark blue *dirndl* with a blouse edged with blue
broidery to match the border of the pleated white apron.

"Yes, it is," agreed Jane, assuming that Mrs. Wroxham was
inking how fetching her daughters would look in miniature
rndls.

"And I think it's the right size," continued Mary. "Dear
e, I've forgotten already how to say – 'May I try it on?' Can
ou remember?"

"I think it's *Darf ich das anprobieren*."

"What a good memory you have. Mine is like a sieve, alas."
Mary turned to the saleswoman and repeated the phrase, at the
ame time indicating that it was not she but Jane who wished
o try the dress.

At this, Jane said with real firmness that she could not af-
ord the *dirndl*.

"It's a present," Mary told her, equally firmly. "A small
onus to thank you for being such a help to me."

"But you're paying me to help you," Jane protested.

"Only pin-money, my dear. And most of the holiday help-
s I've had in the past have not been a quarter as useful as you
e. You see what needs doing, and get on with it without hav-
g to be told. All the other girls needed supervising, and if one
going to supervise, one might just as well do things oneself.
hen we first saw these folk dresses in Freudenstadt, I made
p my mind to give you one."

Her praise brought a flush to Jane's cheeks, and gave her
warm inward glow.

Towards the end of the afternoon, when his sister was de-

"Yes, thank you. We went to the Rheinfall. It was lovely –
until the rain started. Have you had a good day?"

"Today I have visited Zürich, and there also it has rained,"
he told her, with a rueful grimace. "To camp when it rains
is not pleasant." He paused. "To camp *alone* is not pleasant,"
he went on, more vehemently. "Here, everyone is with friends.
Only I am not with friends. For three days I have had no conversation." Again he paused. "You do not mind that I speak
to you? My English is not so good."

"Your English is excellent," said Jane. "Where is your
home?"

"I am from Delft in Holland," he told her. "My name is
Willem ... Willem Hoogveld. Your name I know. I have heard
the children call you Jane."

"Is your tent near ours?"

"There is my tent." He pointed to a small, khaki-coloured
ridge tent on the other side of the caravan next to their van.
"It belongs to my friend Jan who should also be here. But since
two weeks Jan has broken his arm, and so he must stay at
home. As I have arranged to be away from the place where I
work, I come alone. Now I wish very much I had *not* come," he
ended gloomily.

"Yes, it must be miserable all on your own in this weather.
Are you staying at this camp for the whole of your holiday, or
are you moving from place to place?"

"I don't know what is best to do," he said, with a doleful
shrug. "I am not having a good time here. But will it be better
in another place?" He paused. "You and your family? Do you
remain at Waldshut for long?"

"No, not long. We're on our way to the Bernese Alps. The
people I am with are not my family. I'm their holiday help ...
a sort of *au pair*," she added.

"Ah, that explains. I thought the Englishman and his wife
were not the correct age to be your mother and father."

Jane corrected his misunderstanding of David's relationship
to Mary, and explained why her employer's husband was ab-

sent. In turn, she learned that Willem was the youngest son of a Delft shopkeeper, that he lived at home but worked in The Hague where he was a newly-qualified accountant, and that the previous year he had spent his summer holiday in England.

Sorry for him in his loneliness, she encouraged him to talk. He was the kind of young man whom Bettina would have dismissed as "duller than a Victorian curate". Jane found his dullness an agreeable relief from the stimulus – often amounting to strain! – of David's society.

On Monday morning, the hills of Switzerland, across the river, were veiled in rain.

"Oh, dear, this is camping at its worst. I *am* sorry, David," said Mary, when they were having a late breakfast.

Even the children had been reluctant to emerge from the snugness of their *schlafsäcke* (as they referred to their sleeping-bags now), on such a wet, chilly day.

"My dear girl, why apologise to me? It's equally miserable for everyone," he replied, with a philosophical shrug.

"Yes, but you often have to endure rather wretched living conditions when you're overseas. It's a shame for you to have to put up with them on your home leave. If you hadn't agreed to take Peter's place, you might be basking on the Riviera now."

"It may be pouring there, too."

"At worst you could be having breakfast in bed in a comfortable hotel."

After breakfast, Jane dealt with the dishes in one of the stainless steel sinks in the special washing-up verandah between the camp laundromat and the women's showers. She had put a ten-pfennig coin in the sink meter, and was watching hot water gush into her plastic bucket when Willem Hoogveld walked past on his way to the men's showers. Seeing her, he stopped to talk for a few minutes. No sooner had he departed than a sardonic voice said, "Well, well! A friendship is blos-

soming, I see. When did you two become a[...] night, presumably. So that's why you didn't [...] the café? You had another fish to fry."

Without glancing over her shoulder, Jane [...] wanted to go to bed early – which I did! I [...] Hoogveld for about fifteen minutes. There's n[...] shouldn't talk to the other campers, is there?"

"Not to my knowledge." David picked up the [...] began to dry the plates she was placing on the dra[...] he told you his first name? 'Mr. Hoogveld' seem[...] in this free-and-easy atmosphere. What is he? A D[...]

"Yes. His first name is Willem."

"Like him?"

"I don't know him well enough to say. Did you [...] you were talking to at the Rheinfall yesterday?"

"In other circumstances, I would probably hav[...] our acquaintance," he answered lazily.

Edward came running up to tell him that Mary wan[...]

"Okay. You help Jane finish here, will you?" Da[...] the towel to his nephew, and strode away, leaving Jan[...] der what he meant by "other circumstances". She ca[...] conclusion that it must be the lack of a car which wa[...] ing his style.

The morning chores finished, David took charge o[...] dren while the women went to Waldshut to replace Ja[...] ing clothing. Had Jane gone shopping alone, she w[...] replaced, as cheaply as possible, the garments she [...] But Mary had other ideas. Clearly she felt this to b[...] opportunity to correct Jane's lamentable lack of dr[...] and since the matching separates which she urged Ja[...] were not expensive, and formed a far more comp[...] wardrobe than the unrelated clothes which had be[...] was difficult to argue with her.

Jane did protest that she had lost only one cotton [...] did not need two tops in its place, or the white-fri[...] wool poncho which Mary advised as a substitute for

bating what to have for supper, David said, "No reflection on your cooking, Mary, but I think it's time we tried the local food. I was talking to a chap in the washroom this morning who has several excellent meals at a *gasthof* at Kadelburg. It's a village a few miles from here. Thomas can go to bed at his usual time. He won't come to any harm, sleeping in the van in the car-park while the rest of us eat. It's been a fairly dismal day. A night out will cheer us up."

"I think it's a splendid suggestion," she agreed enthusiastically. "It will also give us a chance to get out of trousers and into tights for a few hours."

Later, in the washroom, while the two little girls were sharing a shower, Mary watched Jane brushing her thick hair, and said suddenly, "You can tell me to mind my own business if you like, but I think you scrape your hair back too tightly. Would you allow me to do it as I think it would suit you?"

"Yes . . . if you wish," Jane said doubtfully.

"You can change it back if you don't like it." Mary took the brush and set to work. When she had finished, instead of being pulled back in an ordinary tail, Jane's glossy hair was smoothed round the back of her head and secured behind her left ear, with the tail coming forward over her shoulder.

"These will need to 'set' for a few minutes," said Mary, as she pinned into place, and lightly sprayed, a curl in front of either ear. The effect, when these tendrils were released, was astonishingly different from the severity of Jane's usual hairstyle.

Emerging rosily from the shower cabinet, Emma and Francesca noticed and approved the difference immediately. So even if she had wished to do so – and, deep down, did she? – it would have been churlish, Jane felt, to alter Mrs. Wroxham's handiwork.

Thomas was already fast asleep when they set out for the inn at Kadelburg and, in order not to disturb him, they passed the short journey in silence. It was raining again, so Jane's *dirndl* was concealed by her raincoat, her hair by a cotton kerchief knotted under her chin. She wondered what David would think of her changed appearance. Perhaps he would not notice.

There was not much parking space to spare in the courtyard of the Gasthof zum Oschen when they arrived. "Perhaps we should have booked a table by telephone," said Mary. "How disappointing if we can't get in."

But although a hum of talk and laughter, and the mingled fragrances of good food, cigars and coffee greeted their entrance into the cheerful, wood-panelled dining-room which lay immediately within the small draught lobby, the restaurant had one or two tables free.

It took a few minutes for everyone to divest themselves of their rainwear. Then a waitress showed them to a table with chairs for six people, and indicated that she could soon lay a seventh place. While she was fetching an extra chair, Mary directed her sons to sit opposite their sisters while she and Jane faced each other, leaving the end place for David.

It was Edward who, when everyone was seated, drew attention to Jane by noticing her decorative apron, and asking, "Is that a real pinny? Can you take it off?"

"No, it doesn't untie. It's sewn on," she told him.

He said, with nine-year-old candour, "I like that dress much better than your other one. I think it's a good thing it is lost. It was a horrid colour."

"Edward, that's not polite," said his mother. "You may say when you like things, but you should keep your dislikes to yourself or you may hurt people's feelings."

"But Jane told us that *she* didn't much like her Oxfam dress," said Emma quickly. The twins were always swift in each other's defence.

David lifted an eyebrow. "A what-sort-of dress?"

"From an Oxfam shop," his niece enlightened him. "You must have noticed them, Uncle David. They sell all kinds of funny old things to raise money for people who are starving.

John bought his stuffed owl at an Oxfam shop, and we always buy our Christmas cards there, don't we, Mummy?"

"You're out of touch, David," said his sister. "Most large towns have not one but several Oxfam shops, and they're one of the sources of pre-war fur coats and the Art Deco buckles and brooches which are so fashionable with Jane's generation at present."

"Really? I've heard about Art Nouveau, but Art Deco is something new to me."

"It applies to the fashions and furnishings between the wars, especially of the 1920s," Mary explained. "I think they're hideous, but perhaps —"

She stopped as the waitress, who had darted away to attend to the people at another table, returned to take David's order. While the discussion about food was going on, Jane sat in silence, pierced by an acute disappointment because David had said nothing about her dress or hair. He had noticed them, she knew. Why had he made no remark?

It had been settled that the three grown-ups would try the Zigeuner schnitzel while the children played safe with pork chops, when another large party of holidaymakers entered the *gasthof*. During the bustle of their arrival, David said suddenly to Jane, "Is this what's known as a kiss curl?" And he touched the curling lock of hair in front of her ear, his fingertips brushing her cheek.

It was said in a tone, and with a look, which was not unfamiliar to her. But seeing him watch someone else with that appreciative gleam had not prepared her for the full effect of finding it directed upon herself. Whereas minutes ago her spirits had sagged with disappointment, now they soared to a dizzying peak of elation. For a moment, but only for a moment, nothing mattered but the intense pleasure of looking attractive to the man whose attraction for her she could no longer deny.

Behind him, the lobby door opened yet again.

"Oh, look, the young man from our camp," said Mary. "But

69

he's left it too late, I'm afraid. There are no tables left."

David glanced over his shoulder to where Willem Hoogveld was surveying the now crowded dining-room.

"Perhaps that was the idea," he murmured. "Shall I ask him to join us?"

"By all means," said Mary. "If the table is pulled away from the wall, there's room for him at the end between Edward and Emma."

"No, I'll go there," answered David. "He can take this place, next to Jane. That, no doubt, is the object of the exercise," he added, as he stood up.

His sister, who was speaking to the children, missed this remark. Jane, when she grasped what he meant, came down from her cloud with a bump. Could he really believe that the young Dutchman's arrival was not mere chance? That she and Willem had planned this turn of events? At first the discovery that he thought her capable of such devious tactics made her angry. But almost at once she realised that, even if the idea of such a strategy was repugnant to her, it was much better for David to think that than to guess that *he* was responsible for her transformation.

Thus it was that, as the two men came to the table, her smile for Willem was as brilliant as if David's surmise had been correct.

CHAPTER III

DURING dinner Willem, who after their first conversation by the river had left Jane with the impression of a somewhat diffident personality, surprised her by proving an unexpectedly convivial addition to the party. Indeed it was not long before they were all in festive spirits, for the good food, the wine, and the cosy atmosphere of the inn were all doubly pleasurable after the wet and chilly day.

"But on my radio I hear that tomorrow it will be very hot," Willem told Mary.

"Really? Oh, I do hope so," she answered fervently.

He turned to Jane. "I see you have bought a peasant dress. Such dresses look best when the waist is slim. Sometimes they are worn by persons who are not slim. But on you it looks most pleasing."

"Thank you," said Jane, wondering if from the other end of the table David had heard the compliment, and was eyeing her with a sardonic quirk at the corner of his mouth.

Francesca was half asleep when David called for the bill. Willem, after asking the waitress to make out a separate bill for him, thanked Mary for allowing him to join them. "It is not yet late. You permit Jane to return to the camping in my car, and to drink with me at the café?" he enquired.

Before Mary could reply, David said, "I think not. We want to make an early start tomorrow. Jane needs a good night's sleep."

Willem's fair skin turned brick red. Clearly he had asked Mary's permission only out of politeness, and was taken aback and embarrassed by David's rather snubbing veto. For a moment it looked as if Mary might intercede for him. But while

71

she was visibly hesitating, Willem said a chagrined good night and left the table.

It was not until they were in the van, on the road back to Waldshut, that Mary said, "That was rather arbitrary, wasn't it, David? Perhaps Jane would have liked to drive home with Willem."

Without taking his eyes off the road, her brother said, "Would you have liked it, Jane?"

"Do my wishes matter?" she asked stiffly.

"Answer the question: Did you want to go with him?"

"If you'd given me the chance, I would have made that clear at the time. It's irrelevant now," she retorted.

He gave a short laugh. "He should have asked you in the first place – or told me to mind my own business. He hasn't much gumption, that lad. He likes the way you look in that goose-girl outfit, but he wouldn't like it when he found out that you're a Women's Lib fighter in disguise."

"If there were more men like Willem, and fewer like you, the Women's Lib movement wouldn't be necessary," Jane informed him hotly.

The words had no sooner burst from her than she regretted them. Had they been alone, her outburst would not have mattered. But with Mary and the children present, she should have refused to be provoked.

"I'm sorry, Mrs. Wroxham," she murmured contritely.

"No need to apologise, my dear. I'm inclined to agree with you." Mary seemed more amused than put out.

Later, when they were settling down in their bunks, she asked, "*Would* you have liked to go with Willem?"

"Not particularly," Jane admitted. "But I would rather you didn't tell your brother that."

"I won't," Mary promised. She turned out the light. "I think knowing you will be a salutory experience for David. Most girls eat out of his hand. An acquaintance with one who doesn't will be very good for him." She yawned. "Good night."

"Good night," Jane answered, with a sigh. If only Mary

knew the truth, she thought, as she lay watching the fluttering shadow of a willow frond on the moonlit curtain.

It seemed so unfair that, having successfully kept her emotions in a state of deep-freeze throughout her two years at university, in spite of being surrounded by young men of her own generation, she should find herself thawing to a man who was not only ten years her senior, but unsuitable in every way.

The weather forecast which William had heard on his radio proved to be an accurate one. The following day was hot. At half-past ten they crossed the Rhine bridge into Switzerland. By lunch time they were at Lucerne, on the shore of the Vierwaldsättersee – the Lake of the Four Forest Cantons.

As soon as they arrived in the city, they felt an atmosphere of gaiety and opulence. The streets streamed with expensive cars, the pavements were crowded with well-dressed people, and on the balconies and terraces of the flower-decked luxury hotels overlooking the lake, the very rich tourists basked in cushioned cane chairs, sipping aperitifs and watching the world go by.

Mary had heard that the Lido camping ground, on the outskirts of Lucerne, was among the best in Europe. It was screened from the road by a high green beech hedge. When they drove through the gateway a camp official was waiting to greet them, to explain the booking-in procedure, and to point out which parts of the grounds were for caravanners and auto-campers, and which for tenters.

In spite of the size of the site, and their early arrival, there was not a great choice of vacant spaces. Clearly this camp was always full up by nightfall. Indeed, compared with the three much smaller camps where they had stayed so far, this one seemed over-full, with tents pitched so close together that their pegs and guy-ropes overlapped.

The children were delighted by the crowded bustle of the place. It had everything to please them; a shop selling sweets and ices, a chip stall with a spit on which succulent-looking chickens were roasted, and a maze of tall hedges, ideal for hide and seek and for escaping the surveillance of the grown-ups. Secretly, Jane took an instant dislike to the camp, and thought wistfully of the peaceful meadows and orchards they had seen on the way. But she was careful to hide her opinion.

When John unrolled his sleeping bag, he found an ant in it. "Little does he know that he's in a different country now," he remarked, as he shook the insect to the floor.

It was David who, some moments later, noticed Francesca's woebegone look.

"What's the matter, tuppence?"

"He'll be lost."

"Who?"

"That poor little ant. He'll never find his way home, and perhaps the ants here won't like him. Perhaps they'll *kill* him!"

"Oh, rot. You are a twit, Fanny –" her brother began unsympathetically.

He was silenced by a glance from David who went down on one knee beside her, and said seriously, "I don't think they'll hurt him, Francesca, or that you need worry about him. For all we know he may not have lived at Waldshut. He may make a habit of moving around in people's baggage. He may be a travelling ant, the way I'm a travelling man."

She leaned against his leg. "*Do* ants travel?"

"Why not? Birds migrate. Salmon swim long distances. Why shouldn't an ant have adventures?"

How nice he could be when he chose, Jane thought involuntarily. But was he ever like this with grown-up girls? Somehow she doubted it.

Although it could not be seen from the camp, the lake was close by, and they spent the afternoon in the Lido pleasure grounds, swimming and sunning. Not surprisingly, the lake water was too cold for prolonged bathing. After five minutes in it, Jane began to feel shivery. To whip up her circulation, she swam out to one of the plastic diving floats which were moored in deep water. She was lying in the shallow bowl of the

74

float, feeling much warmer after the burst of strenuous exercise, when she heard another swimmer approaching. Assuming that it was Mary, she did not bother to sit up, or even to open her eyes. So it was with a start of surprise that she heard David saying, "May I join you?" and opened her eyes to find him coming aboard by the ladder.

She sat up and glanced shorewards. Mary was prone on a towel, with Thomas nearby digging a hole in the coarse sand. The other children were capering about on the grass between the beach and the long row of changing cubicles. Jane wondered why David had chosen to join her, instead of sunbathing alongside his sister.

"Pity we can't see the full view," he said, indicating the thick haze veiling the mountains surrounding the lake. "But at least it's warm – out of the water! I can't say I'm keen on the camp here. I prefer fewer people and more elbow room. How about you?"

"Yes, it does seem on the crowded side," she agreed casually. How absurd to be so pleased by the discovery that for once they were in accord. "What does it say on the notice over there?" Earlier she had seen him reading it.

"Oh, it's a warning about the *föhn* . . . the south wind. If the alarm lights round the lake start to flash forty times a minute, it's a signal to people in boats to be on the alert. If the storm warning speeds up to ninety flashes, everyone has to head for the nearest mooring as fast as possible. The *föhn* can beat up some pretty big waves, I believe."

"Where did you learn your German?" she asked. "At school?"

"No, I bought a Linguaphone course to occupy my spare time on a job in Bolivia some years ago. Picking up languages from records is one of the few practical pastimes in my occupation. Air travel prevents one from taking an adequate supply of books on a long assignment in a remote area, and card games have never appealed to me much."

"How many languages can you speak?"

"I'm no linguist," he said, with a shrug of wet brown shoulders. "I can manage a simple conversation in five or six languages, I suppose. But I wouldn't claim to speak any of them fluently. Anyway, once you've tackled a couple of languages, the rest are relatively easy, particularly if one is living among people who speak only Italian or Spanish or whatever." He paused to watch a motor-boat spinning across the lake, some distance away. "Major engineering and mining projects tend to be international operations these days – at least at crew level," he continued presently.

As he talked about his work, Jane relaxed. For once he was treating her as an intelligent being whose age and sex had no relevance to the conversation. Being relaxed and consequently less aware of his manner and more attentive to the matter of what he was saying, she realised from some oblique clues that he must be a man of considerable authority in his field.

It was partly her own fault that eventually this pleasant hiatus came to an end. David had been saying that he considered himself fortunate to be free of the lifelong burden of mortgages, credit repayments and heavy insurances which shackled so many of his contemporaries.

Unthinkingly, Jane remarked, "But don't you ever feel the need for a place of your own ... somewhere in the world which is yours?"

He had been following the progress of a steamer, but the question made him turn to look at her, and at once she knew that she had said the wrong thing.

"No, never," he answered. "That's the point I was making. A place of one's own – and all the possessions and commitments which go with it – can be a prison rather than a haven. I prefer to see and enjoy as much of the world as I can." He paused, and even before he added the rider there was a glint in his eyes which made her uneasy. "There are times when I wouldn't mind having a woman of my own; but I think the kind of woman I have in mind is an almost extinct species."

Suddenly the raft seemed much smaller, the beach much

76

further away, and the man beside her much closer.

"What kind of woman is that?" she asked, trying to sound perfectly casual. "One whose only interest is looking after you, I imagine?"

"You will have to break this unscientific habit of fitting the facts to your theories, instead of adjusting your theories to suit the facts," he told her mildly.

"I don't understand you."

"Fact One: I don't need a woman to look after me in the way you mean. I can cook a meal and wash a shirt as well as you can. Better, I shouldn't wonder."

"*Uncle David ... Yoohoo ... Uncle David!*"

He turned to look shorewards. On the beach, the children were waving and beckoning to him.

"Coming back?" he asked Jane.

"I think I'll sunbathe a little longer."

His dive left the float rocking gently. Jane watched him swimming a leisurely crawl to the beach, his arms coming up and over with a strong, easy stroke, lovely to watch. His departure left her both relieved and disappointed. Now, probably, she would never learn for what kind of woman he might be prepared to give up, not all, but a certain measure of his freedom.

About four o'clock, Mary said, "I don't know what time the shops close here. They may stay open late. In case they don't, I think we should make tracks for town."

"I'll get the van while you and the kids are changing," said David. "I'll pick you up outside the turnstile in about ten minutes. Okay?"

The centre of Lucerne was even more lively than it had been earlier in the day when, presently, a parking place found, they joined the two-way throng of people crossing the mouth of the River Reuss by way of a long, roofed, wooden bridge. It was not difficult to distinguish the tourists crossing the Kapellbrucke from the residents of Lucerne. The locals were the people looking where they were going, and tolerantly avoiding collisions with the tourists, nearly all of whom were gazing roofwards at the strange, often macabre paintings fixed to the beams overhead.

The northern end of the bridge led into the heart of the shopping centre, where even the boys were fascinated by the amazing range of clocks and watches to be seen in the multitude of jewellers' shops.

"Mummy, you *must* see this. . ."

"Jane, how much is four hundred and sixty francs in English money?"

With the exception of Thomas, now being carried astride David's hip, the children darted from window to window, urging their slower elders to come and see each fresh marvel of ingenuity. Ball watches, pendant watches, tiny watches disguised as rings, cheap "fun" watches, fabulously expensive chronometers; there seemed to be as great a variety of watches as of visitors looking at them.

"What would you buy, Jane, if money was no object?" asked David, when at one particularly spectacular display, the others had each picked out the object they considered to be the most covetable.

Jane's gaze ranged over the contents of the window for the second time. "I don't think I would choose anything here."

"Not even that?" He tapped the plate glass with his knuckles, indicating the centrepiece, a collar of emeralds set in textured gold.

"Least of all that. Although I suppose it would be the best choice if one could sell it, and spend the money on things which one really longed for."

"For example?"

She reflected for a moment. "I did once see a piece of jewellery which I would have liked to buy. It was a Victorian brooch of very dark red coral, carved in the form of a hand, with a silver lace cuff. That's the kind of thing I shall look out for, when I can afford it."

"You think in terms of buying for yourself, I notice. Would

78

you disapprove of being given jewels? Is it against your feminist principles?" For once, his tone was not teasing. He sounded genuinely curious.

"No, but I can't imagine anyone giving me jewels."

"I don't see why not. If coral is what you like, a man in love with you would have no problems. You can imagine being loved, can't you?"

They had moved away from the window which had prompted this conversation, and were strolling on, separated from the other members of the family but surrounded by other people. Yet, in spite of the crowd around them, Jane's throat constricted with exactly the same nervous dryness which she had experienced earlier, on the diving raft.

"I – I've never given it much thought."

He gave her a look full of scepticism and amusement, and she turned away, pretending an interest in the windows of a dress shop.

Soon they came to a charming old square, the Weinmarkt, where everyone reassembled to admire the fairy-tale paintings on the façades of the houses round the square, and the lovely Renaissance fountain at its centre.

"I think Lucerne would be a nice place for a honeymoon," Mary remarked.

David said, "Isn't anywhere that?"

His sister smiled. "Yes, in theory even a boarding house in Bootle should be paradisaic. In practice, I think romantic surroundings are an advantage." She turned to Jane. "Peter and I went to Carcassonne, much to the amazement of our friends and relations, most of whom had only the vaguest idea where it was."

"Isn't it that old French town with the high wall all round it, and the pointed turrets?" asked Jane.

"Yes, that's the place. It's supposed to be the most perfect surviving example of a medieval fortress-city. But that isn't quite why we went there. There was a photograph of Carcassonne in one of my textbooks at school, and I'd always

79

wanted to see it. Peter wanted to go because he's a great fan of Ernest Hemingway, and Hemingway used to stay at the Hotel de la Cité in Carcassonne on his journeys to and from Spain. He considered it one of the most beautiful hotels in the world."

"Did you agree with him?" Jane asked her.

"Yes – emphatically! We were there in the early spring when there weren't too many other tourists, and it was like staying in Camelot, especially by moonlight."

"I don't think Jane is as romantic as you are, Mary," David said lazily. "Her idea of a perfect honeymoon is probably two weeks among the archives at the British Museum or, to be really exotic, a fortnight in the Vatican Library."

"Ignore him, my dear," Mary said comfortably. "If he doesn't buck up he'll find he has missed his chance, and there's nobody left who wants to share *his* belated honeymoon," she added, winking at Jane. "Older men are only acceptable if they're rich, my dear David. All *you* have to offer is a life of gypsying around in uncomfortable places like Patagonia and Peru."

"Very true. I'm not a good catch," he agreed carelessly. "On the other hand, what do most girls have to offer which is worth a life share in even my modest income? Running a home for a man is regarded as frustrating drudgery, and going to bed with him is something they're willing to do anyway."

"Nonsense, David. *What* a wild generalisation!" Mary objected, quite crossly. "And a most unsuitable topic with the children around," she added, as Emma hurried up to say that there was an ice-cream place round the corner, and might they have some Swiss money, please?

David bought ices for everyone, and then, for a time, the party re-grouped, and Jane's companion was Francesca. When Mary had finished her shopping, they made their way back to the van by another bridge which also had painted panels and, half way across, a small chapel.

It was when they had re-crossed the river, and Jane was looking in a bookshop, that David came up behind her, and

80

said, "Mary has taken me to task for making remarks unfit for the ears of her offspring, and for your ears, too. I wouldn't have thought what I said was particularly shocking, but anyway I apologise."

"I wasn't shocked. I think you're wrong," she said quietly.

"Do you?" he said, looking down at her.

She coloured under his scrutiny. What were the thoughts behind that intent regard which seemed to penetrate her mental privacy with ease, yet gave no clue to whatever was passing through his mind?

"You're blushing," he said, very quietly, as if they were somewhere secluded from noise and bustle.

The mockery in his eyes, and the oddly disturbing softness of his tone, made Jane's cheeks redder than ever. For the third time that afternoon, she felt all her poise desert her, and realised how helpless she was when he chose to exert this curious power which was like a current flowing between them, causing all sorts of disturbing sensations inside her.

"I believe *you* are almost as innocent as that absurd girl Catherine Morland," he said, with slight emphasis on the "you", and a laugh in his voice. "I've been wondering who you reminded me of."

Her eyes widened. "Catherine Morland in *Northanger Abbey*?"

"Yes. Why? – Are you offended by such a comparison?"

"No ... merely surprised that you've read it." Her confusion was forgotten in her astonishment that a man like David should have read a novel by Jane Austen, her own favourite author, with sufficient attention to recall the name of its heroine.

"You still don't give me much of a rating for intelligence, do you?" he remarked dryly.

They started to walk along in the wake of the others who, now, were almost out of sight.

"It isn't that: I just wouldn't have thought Jane Austen was your kind of writer, any more than Tolstoy is mine. Have you

read *all* her books?"

Her question remained unanswered. They were crossing a road as she asked it and, at that moment, a car swerved round the corner and David's speedy reaction was all that saved her from being struck.

He did not swear, but his grey eyes were momentarily fierce as he stood on the pavement, holding Jane's shoulders to steady her. After the first second or two, it was not the shock of the incident which made her tremble, but the sudden, acute awareness that this was how he might hold her if he meant to kiss her.

With an effort, she found her voice, "Th—that was a near miss! Thank you."

"Are you all right? Did I hurt you, grabbing you like that?"

"I'm glad you did. I may be a little bit bruised, but not nearly as much as I would have been, if you hadn't."

An old man, who evidently had witnessed the incident, approached and spoke to them in Schwyzerdütsch. David dropped his hands from her shoulders, and the two men engaged in a short conversation.

The Wroxhams, when they caught up with them, were leaning on the rails along the riverside, watching a family of ducks bobbing on the rapid current. In the van, going back to the camping, Jane sat in the rear and looked at the back of David's head.

Remembering his reference to *Northanger Abbey*, she found herself thinking how much easier it must have been to live in Jane Austen's time, almost two hundred years ago, when all a girl's hopes and plans were connected with marriage, and there was no troublesome conflict between her emotions and her intellectual ambitions.

I believe you are almost as innocent as that absurd girl Catherine Morland, he had teased her, little guessing that there was no need for the qualifying "almost". Although, unlike Catherine, she was not ignorant as well as innocent, her experience was equally limited.

There were two surprises in store for them when they re-

turned to the camping ground. The first was the disagreeable discovery that the red tent which, earlier, had been next to theirs was there no longer. Their new neighbours were a group of scruffy-looking people who, in defiance of the large sign at the entrance to the camp, were playing a transistor radio.

"Oh, dear!" murmured Mary, dismayed.

The second surprise was a pleasant one.

Someone said, "Good evening, Jane," and they turned to find Willem Hoogveld standing nearby.

"Willem! What are you doing here?" asked Jane, in astonishment.

"After you had gone away this morning, I decided also to visit Lucerne. You do not mind that I follow you?" – addressing this question to Mary.

"No, of course not, Willem. I only wish that you had taken the space next to us," she added, in a discreet undertone. "I don't like the look of that lot."

He followed her apprehensive glance. "Oh, yes – the hippies," he murmured. "I thought you would not be pleased to find such people near to you."

"Where's your tent?" Jane enquired.

"It is the other side of the trees" – waving a hand at the hedge.

Mary invited Willem to share their supper. She had decided to buy three chickens from the camp's spit-roaster, and eight boxes of hot chips – nine now that Willem was joining them.

It was while she was buying this "instant" supper, accompanied by the twins to help her carry it back to their pitch, that she fell into conversation with another Englishwoman, and was invited, later in the evening, to join an impromptu party in the caravanners' part of the camping ground.

"You're included in the invitation, David," she said, telling the rest of the family what had happened. "You don't mind being left out, I hope, Jane? I gather it's a party for middle-agers. What are your plans, Willem? Are you going into town to see what the night life is like?"

"No, tonight I think not. Perhaps tomorrow. Tonight, if you permit, I will talk to Jane."

"I wish you would keep her company, in case that lot become too rowdy" – with a significant nod in the direction of their unwelcome neighbours.

" 'That lot' are preparing to go out," remarked David.

"Are they? Good. Jane and Willem will be able to chat in peace."

"Hm," murmured David, catching Jane's eye with a most sardonic gleam in his own.

She pretended not to notice, and busied herself with helping Mary to serve the supper.

After the meal, Mary decided to have a hot shower and change into something more festive than the blue denim safari suit which she had been wearing all day.

"That was unusually quick," said her brother, when she returned within twenty minutes of setting out. He was only just back from his own shower.

"I haven't been showering. I've been queueing," she informed him. "The wash place is packed with women. There won't be a shower free for ages. I'll have to make do with a basin wash." Her frown changed to a reminiscent grin. "I kept my bikini on, but the girl next to me had no inhibitions. At least not until the door opened and a little old man shuffled in to empty the ash trays and litter bins. I should think you could hear her shriek from here."

"There's a little old lady who cleans the men's loos," said John. "She bustles about all the time. I don't think she notices the campers. She's too busy mopping the floor. It's terrifically clean."

"The women's place isn't," said Mary, making a face. "But that's mainly the fault of the campers, not the camp staff. In my opinion, this camp is too big and too crowded, and some of the people here – not only our neighbours! – are visibly unfussy in their habits."

By nine o'clock a quiet had fallen over the camping. Many

campers had gone to Lucerne. Some were already in bed. The remainder were taking leisurely strolls around the paths, or were sitting outside their tents, talking in lowered tones, or reading by the light of bottled-gas lamps.

At ten, Willem said good night, and Jane went to bed. At eleven David and Mary returned. A couple of hours later they, and everyone else in the vicinity, were woken up by the uproarious return of the people on the next pitch.

"For heaven's sake! Are they drunk?" exclaimed Mary, slipping out of her bunk, and leaning across Jane's to draw back the curtain and see what was happening outside.

If, as seemed likely, their neighbours had imbibed too freely during their outing, they soon sobered up when a tall figure emerged from the Wroxhams' tent.

David's comments on their inconsiderate behaviour were voiced too quietly for Jane and Mary to catch what he had to say. But there must have been steel in his tone. The effect was immediate. The "hippies", as Willem had termed them, quietened as swiftly and completely as rowdy children who are called to order by someone who they sense will not stand any nonsense.

Wearing only pyjama trousers, with no jacket to conceal, if not the breadth of his shoulders, the superb fitness which even Jane had failed to recognise before Sonsfeld, David looked more than a match for the two large but out-of-condition males from the neighbouring tent.

The following morning the mountains were still invisible, but Mary felt they should plan an expedition, buy provisions for a picnic lunch, and hope that the mist would clear during the day.

After she and David had had a conclave inside the van, she said, "Come on, all of you. Hurry up and get ready. We're going to make an early start. We can buy the bread and anything else we need at our first stopping place. I think you'd better spend a penny, darling" – holding out her hand to her youngest son.

Presently, Emma noticed Willem approaching.

"We're going on a Mystery Tour," she informed him.

"I know. Your mother is very kind; she has asked me to come with you."

The children were pleased. They liked the young Dutchman. But, observing David's expression at that moment, Jane deduced that he did not.

Later, when Mary returned, she heard him murmur to his sister, "Won't it be rather cramped with four adults aboard?"

"I don't think so. Anyway, it would have been unkind to leave him on his own all day."

Since Willem was clean, tidy, polite, conventional in his choice of clothes and with nothing about him calculated to antagonise a man of an older generation, Jane found David's dislike puzzling.

Although, when they first set out, there seemed little hope of the weather improving, they had not gone many kilometres before shafts of sunlight began to penetrate gaps in the clouds. The road skirted the lakeside, sometimes low down by the water's edge, and sometimes hundreds of feet above it where the route was literally a highway carved in the face of the precipice. When, for the third time, they stopped in one of the special flower-bedded, safety-railed laybys which the Swiss had created at the finest vantage points, the sunlight had become so warm that it was necessary to shed the woollies in which they had begun the excursion.

"Ah . . . this is more like it," said Mary gratefully.

In the little town of Schwyz, she bought bread, and John and the twins clubbed together for a cow bell which, as they chose it from a selection in an ironmongery shop, cost only twelve francs, much less than a similar bell from a souvenir shop.

Considering that Schwyz was not a large place, some of the old houses were surprisingly palatial. David said this was because, in earlier centuries, the men of Schwyz had been particularly fine soldiers, and had made fortunes serving in foreign armies. Those who survived and came home had put their money into mansions.

It was David who knew that the reason the Swiss children were already back at school was because they would have an extra "potato" holiday in the autumn, and a week off for winter sports in February.

When it was time for lunch, he parked the van in a layby and they scrambled up the slippery turf of a steep, wooded slope to a spot where the road was out of sight, and where there was nothing to be seen but the forested heights on the other side of the valley, and the summits of the mountains all about them.

Seated on massive slabs of sun-baked rock, they ate a simple but ambrosial meal of crusty bread with butter, cheese, salami and hard-boiled eggs.

"Isn't this lovely?" said Mary, sighing with pleasure. "If only Peter could be here. I must telephone him tonight, David. I do hope he'll be able to join us for at least one week of the holiday."

"If Daddy comes, will Jane sleep in the tent with us and Uncle David?" asked Francesca.

"If Daddy comes, Uncle David will be able to go to the seaside in France, which was what he meant to do originally," her mother reminded her. "Is that still your intention?" – to her brother.

Before he could reply, Emma said, "Do stay with us, Uncle David. You won't have nearly as much fun, all on your own. There's plenty of room in the tent for Jane *and* Uncle David, Mummy. She could sleep in his part, or she could have our room, and we could share his part."

"We'll cross that bridge when we come to it," Mary said lightly. "Poor old Daddy may not be able to join us at all."

John, who had finished his lunch before anyone else, returned from a scramble up the hillside with a palmful of wild strawberries. The tiny berries were so delicious that everyone went to look for more.

Jane, having charge of Thomas, did not search as far afield as the others. Presently, as the little boy seemed to prefer picking wild flowers to strawberry-hunting, they remained in a small, level glade where at first she sat, and then lay, on the warm grass.

Without Thomas to keep an eye on, she could easily have fallen asleep. Now and then, from further up the hill, she heard the voices of the others. Nearby, Thomas kept up a soft soliloquy, but this was more soothing than disturbing. As long as she could hear him murmuring to himself, she knew he was not straying. The rockier parts of the hill made dangerous climbing for a four-year-old.

When her cheek was stroked with a grass head, she did not open her eyes, but smiled and reached up her hand to capture his plump wrist. The hand which met hers was not small, soft and slightly sticky. It was a masculine hand, and even before she blinked in surprise at its owner, she knew that those long, strong fingers did not belong to Willem.

David released her hand, and sat down on the grass. He was carrying a bottle, two beakers, and a paper bag.

"I bought this wine in Schwyz for our lunch, and then left it behind in the van," he said, extracting the cork with a practised turn of his wrist. "Want some more strawberries, Thomas?"

Thomas trotted up for his share of several ounces of strawberries which his uncle had gathered. Then he pottered away again.

Handing Jane's wine to her, David said, "Your Dutch swain misses his chances. I expected to find him with you, but he's toiling up the hill with the kids."

She sipped the wine, and said mildly, "How you love to tease."

He cocked an eyebrow. "But today you're not going to rise, hm?"

She shook her head. "I'm feeling too lazy."

Presently, looking up at the blue sky and the tall green spires of the firs surrounding the glade, he said, "Emma could be right. Maybe I should forget France. If Richard joins us, I can buy a small hike tent, or perhaps one of those inflatable igloo-shaped things which seem to be popular."

The wine must have gone straight to her head. She only just stopped herself saying, "I wish you would stay with us."

"It's an interesting point of convention that, if we were somewhere with no risk of rain, it would acceptable for the children and you and me to sleep in a glade like this one. But to adopt either of Emma's suggestions would not be acceptable," he said. "At least not from the point of view of my sister and brother-in-law. People of your age don't seem to worry too much about the finer observances."

"Some do, some don't, she replied. "Doesn't it all depend on circumstances? I can't imagine worrying about the conventions if I was stuck on a mountain, in a blizzard, and the only shelter had to be shared with a man."

"Supposing there were two shelters? One occupied by me, and one by young Hoogveld. In whose trust, I wonder, would you feel your reputation was the safest?"

"As I wouldn't be bothered about my reputation in those circumstances, I would shelter with you," answered Jane.

For once, she had the satisfaction of surprising him.

"Really?"

"I'd be more concerned with my survival," she explained. "And obviously you're much better qualified to survive a mountain storm than someone who's always lived in towns."

His lips twitched. "A realist to the bone, aren't you, Jane? No high-flown, romantic notions about death before dishonour for you. My sister, at your age, would undoubtedly have chosen Willem, and imagined herself being found frozen, locked in his arms."

"I doubt if there's anything romantic about dying from exposure," said Jane. "And even if I were as pretty as Helga, I shouldn't think even you would have time for ... for dishonourable intentions in a blizzard."

"Helga?" he said interrogatively.

"Your sister's mother's help the last time you were on leave. I gather you were rather taken with her."

"Oh, Helga . . . yes, I remember. Quite pretty, but not very bright. When you relax and forget to be prickly, you're far more attractive than she was. However, as you say, a night on the bare mountain would tend to damp anyone's ardour – even mine!" He paused. "I wonder why you have me tagged as a philandering type? Apart from once climbing, by accident, into your bedroom, I've done nothing to earn that reputation."

Jane hesitated. "No, but you always behave as if you might . . . given the smallest encouragement," she told him, with unwonted candour.

Rather to her surprise, this made him laugh. He said, with a gleam of devilment, "The day may come, my dear Jane, when you'll wish I had kissed you. In forty years' time, when all this is only a memory –"

"Mum says we should get on, or we won't get home before dark," announced John, bursting into the glade, his fair skin red from exertion, his knuckles grazed, and a rip in one leg of his jeans.

"What happened to you?" asked his uncle, rising, and offering his hand to Jane.

In the safety of John's presence, she accepted a pull to her feet.

"I slipped," the boy answered carelessly. "Oh, you've got some plonk. Can I have a swig?"

"Should he?" asked Jane, as David poured some wine into the beaker he had used.

"It hasn't gone to your head, has it?"

"No, but he looks so hot."

Where the hillside gave way to the road, there was a fairly high retaining wall. John jumped into the roadway, and turned to help his little brother. Then David sprang, handed the wine bottle to John, and waited for Jane who, even without Thomas to look after, had come down the hill more cautiously than the sure-footed males.

There being no courteous way of declining his offered assistance, she was forced to bend forward and rest her palms on David's shoulders which, under his blue cotton shirt, felt as firm as rock. He gripped her waist and swung her down beside him.

John had already shepherded Thomas across the road to the van where the others were waiting. But now a motor coach was coming. As they waited for it to pass, David said, "Well, I'm glad to know that I have your confidence in blizzards, if nowhere else."

The coach went by. As they crossed the road, he added, "But I shouldn't rely too much on lack of encouragement. Girls have been known to put up barricades for the pleasure of having them breached, you know."

From their lunch place, the road wound upwards, higher and higher, nearer and nearer to the glistening, blue-shadowed snowfields.

"Are we nearly there, Mummy? – Wherever it is that we're going?" asked Emma.

"We're crossing the Alps by the Susten Pass, children. Uncle David knows more about it than I do."

David swung the van round a perfectly-cambered hairpin bend before he said, "I've been wanting to see this road for years. It's the first mountain road, expressly designed for motoring, which the Swiss ever built. It's a masterpiece."

Jane, who had never had a good head for heights, had thought about their excursions among the mountains with a certain amount of apprehension. But although the Susten road was not particularly wide, and the bed of the valley was now thousands of feet below, she found she was not at all nervous.

The outer side of the road was lined with stubby granite pillars, which David called *bouteroues*. Beyond these, the hillside sloped before it dropped sharply. There were none of the hair-raising precipices, inches from the wheels of passing

91

vehicles, which she had expected and dreaded, either going up mountains or coming down them.

At the top of the Pass, the roadway entered a tunnel bored through the rock of the summit. Beyond the tunnel was a large, crowded car park, and a flag-decked restaurant with kiosks selling postcards and souvenirs.

Most of the tourists seemed content to admire the views from here. The Wroxhams followed a stony track leading to higher ground, and soon the children were pelting each other with snowballs.

"Doesn't it seem peculiar to be walking on snow, in summer clothes, and to feel hot," remarked Mary, as she and Jane crunched across a small snowfield. "But I daresay it's pretty nippy up here at night. Too cold for camping, unfortunately. How high are we here, David?" raising her voice to reach her brother, some yards away.

"Well over seven thousand feet."

At the level at which they were walking, the landscape resembled rugged moorland, with outcrops of yellow-lichened rock among stretches of turf. The peaks, much closer now, were still mysterious and formidable.

Before they returned to the van, Mary chose several postcards. Jane bought only one, and a stamp, and posted it to Bettina Brooke in Majorca.

"To your boy-friend?" asked Willem, while she was thinking what to write.

"I haven't a boy-friend," she told him. David was not within earshot.

Willem smiled. "I am sure you have many, but I am glad there is no one very important to you. Jane, will you come to Lucerne with me this evening? To eat, and perhaps to dance?"

"It depends what time we get back. Mrs. Wroxham may want to go out with her brother tonight. This holiday is not much fun for her without her husband."

"Yes, I understand. But if it is possible, you will come?"

She hesitated. "I'll see. It's nice of you to ask me."

The second part of the round trip took them over the less high Brunig Pass, and through several peaceful valleys where small country campings of four or five tents in flowery meadows sloping to clear, snow-fed streams made Mary regret that they had to go back to the Lucerne camp.

"We should have packed up and left there this morning," she said, looking enviously at some people having tea outside their caravan. They, and the occupant of a hike tent in the far corner of the same field, were the only visitors to that particular camping which was evidently run by the owner of the nearby farmhouse. A little way along the road, they saw the farmer and all his family busily hay-making.

Jane spent much of the return drive debating whether or not to accept Willem's invitation.

They were approaching the suburbs of Lucerne when David said, "Have you had any thoughts about this evening, Mary? Would the children enjoy a folklore evening? There's one on tonight – yodelling, alpenhorn blowing, flag throwing and so forth."

"Oh, yes, Mummy – please! Do let's go."

Mary, when she learned that the show did not finish until eleven, said firmly that this was much too late for the two youngest children to stay up. "But the rest of you can go," she added. "After I've telephoned Peter, I shall go to bed early and read."

At this, Willem said, "I have asked Jane if she will come with me this evening, but she has not said yes because of thinking you would wish her to guard the children."

"She did that last night. Tonight is her night off," said Mary.

Willem looked enquiringly at Jane. They were both sitting in the rear of the van. Mary was driving, and David was in the front passenger seat with Francesca on his lap.

As Jane hesitated, he turned to look at her, and said, "Well, which is it to be? *Fondue* with Willem, or flag throwing with us?"

93

She knew then, without any doubt, the choice she wanted to make; and she saw that a possible compromise was to suggest that they all went out together. But something in David's expression made her say, "*Fondue* with Willem."

Mary's telephone talk with her husband left her little wiser than before. Doctor Wroxham hoped to be able to join them at the week-end, but was still unable to say definitely that he could.

"I'm to ring him again on Friday night," his wife reported, rather despondently.

As the folklore programme did not begin until half-past eight, David and the older children were having supper in camp with Mary and the two little ones. David was cooking when Willem came to fetch Jane. The young Dutchman had changed into a pale suit with a patterned pink shirt and matching tie. Jane had put on her *dirndl*.

David, who had tied Mary's striped butcher's apron over the clothes he had been wearing all day, contrived to make her feel that she and Willem were over-dressed.

"Have fun," he said to them, and although he had barely glanced at the younger man, she was certain that he was mentally raising his eyebrows at Willem's shirt and tie. Closing her mind to the fact that, at first sight, she herself had thought they were rather unfortunate, Jane told herself it was typical of David's general arrogance to be amused by the mischosen peacock feathers of a much less assured male. Probably he gave minimal thought to his own clothes.

It was luck that his plain cotton shirts and navy wool sweaters – he never wore synthetics, she had noticed – were the kind which looked right in every circumstance, and which suited his tanned, raw-boned looks in a way that pink fancy-weave nylon did not become Willem's present complexion. Their hours in the high mountain sun had been too much, in one day, for his Netherlands blondness.

But the fact that he looked like a lobster, and was clearly self-conscious about it, made Jane warm towards him, and

were
...ree yards from
...ing back to our 'lane' from the
... was bound to see you."

His smallest nephew was tugging at his trouser leg, and he broke off to lift Thomas up to the rim of the balloon car. When, his interest quickly satisfied, the little boy scampered away to inspect something else, David went on, "If you had wanted privacy, there was no shortage of darker, more secluded spots around the camp. But I imagine you didn't want too much privacy in case Hoogveld became over-enthusiastic. Very prudent! Two days isn't exactly old acquaintance," he added dryly.

The hint of censure in his tone made her say defensively, "I'm sure you've often kissed girls on much shorter acquaintance. But of course that's *quite* different! – You're a man!"

From the stairs leading up to another floor, the twins were beckoning excitedly. Jane hurried to join them.

"We've been on television," they told her. "It's round the

feel glad that she had chosen his company rather than David's. How David would have mocked had he known that it was her first date, she thought, as they set out in Willem's car.

It was a pleasant if not memorable evening. At half past eleven, seeing that she was tired, he took her back to the camping.

"Tomorrow, if the others go to the mountains again, perhaps we might spend all day together," he suggested.

"Perhaps," Jane said cautiously. "But this is a working holiday for me. I can't take too much time off. It wouldn't be right. Mrs. Wroxham has been very kind – and generous! – to me."

On the Halden Strasse, a straight stretch of road between central Lucerne and the camping, he took advantage of the absence of much other traffic to remove his right hand from the wheel, and to reach for Jane's hand. It was this which made her start to consider the possibility that, when they came to say good night, he might expect, or feel expected, to kiss her. She did not mind him holding her hand. But, although it might be customary, she was not sure that she wished to participate in what Belinda inelegantly termed "a spot of snogging".

In one way, she would be glad if he kissed her, for then her curiosity about the experience would be satisfied. On the other hand it seemed rather callous to kiss him for that reason only; to make use of him without feeling any special warmth towards him as an individual. She liked him, certainly. But she was not attracted to him, except in the negative sense that nothing about him repelled her.

Willem parked the car near his tent, and they walked round the corner together. It was now about ten minutes to midnight, and there was no light showing through the curtains of the Wroxhams' van, or through the walls of the tent.

"Thank you very much, Willem. It was a nice evening. I enjoyed myself," said Jane, in a low voice.

Whereupon Willem kissed her.

He would have continued to kiss her, but she broke away,

not ungently, and murmured good night.

Next morning, Mary returned from the washroom in a state of considerable irritation. "I had to wait twenty minutes before I could get to a basin!" she exclaimed vexedly. "And most of the girls there weren't washing – they were putting on elaborate eye make-up. Can you understand such total lack of consideration? I wouldn't have the gall to fiddle about with my false eyelashes while other people were waiting to wash their necks and clean their teeth. I've had enough of this place, David. Let's move on to somewhere which isn't so noisy and crowded."

"By all means," her brother agreed. "The sooner the better as far as I'm concerned."

"But, Mum, you said we could go to the Transport Museum today. You promised!" John reminded her.

"Oh, lord – so I did. Do you desperately want to see it, darling? It doesn't sound very exciting to me."

John's face fell. He did not protest, but he looked so profoundly disappointed that Mary said quickly, "But I promised, so of course we'll go. But we'll pack up and pay our bill first, so that as soon as we've seen the museum we can be on our way."

"Where are we heading for this time, Mummy?" asked Edward.

"For our journey's end ... for the Valley of Waterfalls," said his mother.

Willem, when he came to say good morning, and found their tent already dismantled, looked as crestfallen as John had done when he thought he was going to miss seeing the Swiss Institute of Transport and Communication.

"Why don't you come to the Valley of Waterfalls with us?" suggested Emma.

"I wish it were possible. But today is Thursday, and on Sunday night my holiday is finished. While you go south, I must start to travel north," he said regretfully.

"Sorry .
van, his curiosity also forgotten.

Neither Mary nor Jane expected to find the Transpo[...]
Museum particularly interesting.

"But no doubt David and the boys will love it, and spe[...] all day here – if we let them," said Mary, as she followed J[...] through the turnstile at the entrance. The large, modern bu[...] ing with its plate glass walls, shiny floors and wide, o[...] tread staircases seemed more like an air terminal [...] a museum.

As it turned out, although there were a few exhi[...] limited appeal to unmechanically-minded females, th[...] also much to interest and amuse the two women and [...] girls.

Mary had been hustled away to watch her sons t[...] at the controls of an aeroplane-simulator, and J[...] herself, standing on tiptoe to look inside the hu[...] upholstered basket in which a dark-haired, rath[...]

feel glad that she had chosen his company rather than David's. How David would have mocked had he known that it was her first date, she thought, as they set out in Willem's car.

It was a pleasant if not memorable evening. At half past eleven, seeing that she was tired, he took her back to the camping.

"Tomorrow, if the others go to the mountains again, perhaps we might spend all day together," he suggested.

"Perhaps," Jane said cautiously. "But this is a working holiday for me. I can't take too much time off. It wouldn't be right. Mrs. Wroxham has been very kind – and generous! – to me."

On the Halden Strasse, a straight stretch of road between central Lucerne and the camping, he took advantage of the absence of much other traffic to remove his right hand from the wheel, and to reach for Jane's hand. It was this which made her start to consider the possibility that, when they came to say good night, he might expect, or feel expected, to kiss her. She did not mind him holding her hand. But, although it might be customary, she was not sure that she wished to participate in what Belinda inelegantly termed "a spot of snogging".

In one way, she would be glad if he kissed her, for then her curiosity about the experience would be satisfied. On the other hand it seemed rather callous to kiss him for that reason only; to make use of him without feeling any special warmth towards him as an individual. She liked him, certainly. But she was not attracted to him, except in the negative sense that nothing about him repelled her.

Willem parked the car near his tent, and they walked round the corner together. It was now about ten minutes to midnight, and there was no light showing through the curtains of the Wroxhams' van, or through the walls of the tent.

"Thank you very much, Willem. It was a nice evening. I enjoyed myself," said Jane, in a low voice.

Whereupon Willem kissed her.

He would have continued to kiss her, but she broke away,

95

not ungently, and murmured good night.

Next morning, Mary returned from the washroom in a state of considerable irritation. "I had to wait twenty minutes before I could get to a basin!" she exclaimed vexedly. "And most of the girls there weren't washing – they were putting on elaborate eye make-up. Can you understand such total lack of consideration? I wouldn't have the gall to fiddle about with my false eyelashes while other people were waiting to wash their necks and clean their teeth. I've had enough of this place, David. Let's move on to somewhere which isn't so noisy and crowded."

"By all means," her brother agreed. "The sooner the better as far as I'm concerned."

"But, Mum, you said we could go to the Transport Museum today. You promised!" John reminded her.

"Oh, lord – so I did. Do you desperately want to see it, darling? It doesn't sound very exciting to me."

John's face fell. He did not protest, but he looked so profoundly disappointed that Mary said quickly, "But I promised, so of course we'll go. But we'll pack up and pay our bill first, so that as soon as we've seen the museum we can be on our way."

"Where are we heading for this time, Mummy?" asked Edward.

"For our journey's end ... for the Valley of Waterfalls," said his mother.

Willem, when he came to say good morning, and found their tent already dismantled, looked as crestfallen as John had done when he thought he was going to miss seeing the Swiss Institute of Transport and Communication.

"Why don't you come to the Valley of Waterfalls with us?" suggested Emma.

"I wish it were possible. But today is Thursday, and on Sunday night my holiday is finished. While you go south, I must start to travel north," he said regretfully.

"We shall be spending the last two days of our holiday in the Hague. Perhaps we shall meet then, Willem," remarked Mary. "And I will give you our address in case you should come to England again."

She jotted it down on a slip of paper and in exchange he gave her the telephone numbers of his office and his parents' house at Delft.

"It is a shame that Willem can't come with us. I like him," said Emma when, presently, Willem waved them good-bye from the camp gateway.

"Who knows? He may be sufficiently *épris* to go a.w.o.l.," murmured David.

"What does aywoll mean?" enquired Edward, the only one of the children to overhear this remark.

"Absent without leave," said his mother. As he opened his mouth to ask another question, she added briskly, "Edward, you didn't wash properly this morning. Your ears are disgraceful!"

"Sorry . . . I forgot." Edward retreated to the back of the van, his curiosity also forgotten.

Neither Mary nor Jane expected to find the Transport Museum particularly interesting.

"But no doubt David and the boys will love it, and spend all day here – if we let them," said Mary, as she followed Jane through the turnstile at the entrance. The large, modern building with its plate glass walls, shiny floors and wide, open-tread staircases seemed more like an air terminal than a museum.

As it turned out, although there were a few exhibits of limited appeal to unmechanically-minded females, there was also much to interest and amuse the two women and the little girls.

Mary had been hustled away to watch her sons taking turns at the controls of an aeroplane-simulator, and Jane was by herself, standing on tiptoe to look inside the huge, elegantly upholstered basket in which a dark-haired, rather David-like balloonist called Captain Eduard Spelterini had once soared perilously to alp-level, when, behind her, David himself said, "I think it's just as well that young Hoogveld has run out of holiday. He's too naïve to tangle with a girl like you."

She sank to her heels. "What do you mean by that?"

He surveyed the interior of the basket for a moment. "Two things I've always wanted to try . . . ballooning and parachuting," he said absently, as if his previous remark and her question had never been uttered. Then he turned to look at her, his grey eyes disconcertingly alert. "I was an involuntary witness to the end of your evening out. After you'd kissed and left him, Hoogveld practically took root. If I hadn't spoken to him, I think he'd have stood there all night. He was literally entranced, poor devil."

A vivid blush stained her cheeks. "Where were you? Concealed in the bushes? Do you often watch . . . things which are private?"

"There was nothing very private about it, honey. You were slap in the middle of the path, and less than three yards from a lamp standard. Anyone coming back to our 'lane' from the washrooms was bound to see you."

His smallest nephew was tugging at his trouser leg, and he broke off to lift Thomas up to the rim of the balloon car. When, his interest quickly satisfied, the little boy scampered away to inspect something else, David went on, "If you had wanted privacy, there was no shortage of darker, more secluded spots around the camp. But I imagine you didn't want too much privacy in case Hoogveld became over-enthusiastic. Very prudent! Two days isn't exactly old acquaintance," he added dryly.

The hint of censure in his tone made her say defensively, "I'm sure you've often kissed girls on much shorter acquaintance. But of course that's *quite* different! – You're a man!"

From the stairs leading up to another floor, the twins were beckoning excitedly. Jane hurried to join them.

"We've been on television," they told her. "It's round the

precisely that casual 'Why not?' attitude which, demonstrated by my sex, you found so deplorable?"

"I do."

"Which suggests that you had a better reason for kissing Hoogveld."

"I didn't kiss him. He kissed me," she exclaimed, exasperated.

"If you say so . . . but from where I was standing it didn't look as if he was in command of the situation."

Jane was provoked into saying, "I suppose when you kiss a girl she practically faints away with ecstasy?"

"I've never known one to detach herself quite as collectedly as you did last night." David's grey eyes narrowed with unkind amusement. "You look sceptical? Would you like me to substantiate that claim?"

She backed away. "Don't you dare!"

"I dare . . . but I won't," he said lazily. "Frankly, I suspect that the thought of being in my arms has more effect –though perhaps not in the direction of ecstasy – than the act of kissing as performed by your diffident Dutchman. I'll tell you something else. Given a little more time, that boy could have been hurt. He really liked you."

"As I liked him!"

"In passing, merely. As a partner in a harmless holiday flirtation. Harmless to you: perhaps not as harmless to him."

"Whereas you, being almost on a plane with the Chevalier Bayard, would never hold a girl's hand unless your intentions were serious. Of all the hypocritical – "

She stopped short as Emma ran up to them. "Where is Mummy? Oh, here she comes." She darted away towards her mother.

In the few moments before Mary joined them, David said in a low voice, "Curious! I took you for one of those nice, old-fashioned girls to whom a kiss was still something important. Maybe one *should* believe all one reads in the papers about university students."

Upon which remark, he walked away.

Mary seemed not to notice the effect of her brother's parting shot. Or perhaps she noticed the stricken look which Jane was unable to mask, but chose not to make any remark while Emma and Thomas were near.

Afterwards, Jane had only the vaguest memory of the rest of the things in the museum. She recalled seeing a model railway layout of a complexity which John and Edward would have been content to watch until closing time; and she remembered some "retired" steam engines and antique railway carriages. But although they remained in the building for more than an hour from the time when David walked away, for most of that time she was unable to fix her mind on anything but his last words to her.

They had left on her the impression that, despite his frequent mockery of her views, he had liked her more than he let on; but that now she had lost his good opinion. And instead of not caring what he thought, she minded his scorn very much.

Before they left the museum, they had ice-creams and fruit drinks in the *Rigi*, the century-old lake steamer now converted into a café in the courtyard at the heart of the building. Sipping her lemonade, Jane allowed herself one glance at David, and encountered an unfathomable look which made her hurriedly lower her lashes.

CHAPTER IV

THEY reached the small town of Lauterbrunnen, in the long narrow Valley of Waterfalls, at the hottest hour of the afternoon. The Schützenbach camping ground, recommended to Doctor Wroxham by one of his patients, was close to the town, but as Lauterbrunnen consisted of a cluster of geranium-decked chalets, a few homely-looking hotels, and a single shopping street, its proximity to the camp was convenient rather than dismaying.

"All the same, I'll take a look at the washrooms before we commit ourselves," said Mary, as David parked the van.

"Look, Mummy, look! A snow mountain!"

Francesca was the first of the children to see, towering at the head of the valley, the gleaming white peak of the Breithorn.

"Oh, look – there's one of the waterfalls!" This exclamation came from Emma, who was pointing excitedly at the cascade of spray pouring down the face of one of the tremendous precipices which enclosed the valley on both sides.

Only David seemed unimpressed by the spectacular beauty of the canyon. When Mary came back from her reconnaissance inside the camp, and reported that the washroom appeared to be spotless, he said, "I've camped in places like this overseas. You realise that these high cliffs will cut down the hours of sunshine?"

"Surely you're not suggesting that we shouldn't stay here?" she asked, in astonishment.

He shrugged. "It's up to you. I'm merely pointing out a drawback."

"I think it's an idyllic spot. This is how I've always imagined Switzerland in summer. Do you like it, Jane?"

"Yes, it's beautiful."

"Then we'll stay."

Her brother did not argue. Ten minutes later, when they were choosing a place to pitch the tent, he deferred, with another shrug of the shoulders, to Mary's choice of a spot at the edge of the camping field in preference to the more central pitch which he had suggested.

Jane suspected that the truth of the matter was that he had had enough of wholesome family fun, and was becoming restive. What day was it? Wednesday? No, Thursday. How quickly, without newspapers and television, one lost track of time. Although it might seem to her that the holiday had scarcely begun, in fact it would soon be half over.

Probably, to David it seemed high time that it *was* over.

When the tent was up, Mary asked Jane to go to the camp shop for her. The children had already scampered off to explore a nearby thicket of trees.

"I'll come with you and get some beer," said David, when Mary had listed the things she required.

Jane was surprised by this suggestion, for his caustic remarks in the Transport Museum that morning were still stinging her spirit. She had expected him to avoid her company from now on.

The Schützenbach camp shop was well stocked with everything from Camembert to sticking plasters. When David asked for beer, the camp warden hooked a crate of bottles from the stream running only a few yards from the shop counter.

The camp was on two levels separated by a bluff of land about twenty feet high, and connected by a flight of steps. As David and Jane walked back up the sloping unmade road to their pitch on the upper level, a girl stepped out of a caravan and settled down to sunbathe on a canvas lounger.

Her paleness suggested that she had only just started her holiday, but even without a sun-tan, her plump but well-proportioned figure, set off by a yellow bikini (identical to the one for which, in May, Belinda had paid nine guineas), was the kind most people would notice appreciatively.

Certainly David did. "A cuddly armful," he murmured.

As they came within speaking distance of her, the girl smiled. "Hello. You're GBs too, aren't you? Where have you come from today?"

"From Lucerne. And you?" David asked.

"This is our first camp. We – my parents and I – spent last night at a French hotel on our way from Calais to this place. I'm Chloe Brundall."

"This is Jane Winfarthing, and I'm David Carleton."

Jane murmured hello, and added, "Mrs. Wroxham may be waiting for some of these things. Excuse me, Miss Brundall. I'd better get back with them."

As she walked away, she heard Chloe say, "Oh, you're not all one family, then? I didn't think you could be the father of all those children."

When Jane reached the van, Mary asked, "Who is David talking to?"

"An English girl. Chloe Brundall."

"Nice?"

"Very pretty."

"Hm. I think we'll have rice for supper, Jane, with a couple of those tins of chicken in savoury sauce, and a big pan of fried onions. But there's no need to start cooking yet. I'm going to relax for an hour, and gaze at that marvellous mountain. Why don't you do the same? You look tired today. No wonder, with those pile-drivers starting to thump at seven this morning, and foghorns hooting from the lake. Never mind, I'm sure we shall sleep well in this peaceful place."

She arranged two camp chairs to face the Breithorn. For a short time Jane sat beside her. But in the foreground of the view of the snow-covered range at the head of the valley were David and Chloe, still chatting. Try as she might, she could not help watching them. Presently, seeing that Mary was now

105

half asleep, she rose very quietly from her chair and took the laundry bucket to the timber building in the centre of the field which combined a washroom for men, another for women, and, at the back, a laundry equipped with a coin-operated washing machine.

Jane washed, by hand, everything in the bucket, including one of David's shirts, the socks, shirts and shorts the children had worn the day before, and her own and Mary's underwear. As the covered lines outside the laundry were already full, she took the washing back to the tent, intending to peg the lighter articles to the guy-ropes of the entrance canopy.

David, strolling up the driveway which circled the field, said, "I'll fix a linen line for you." He even smiled at her.

Talking to the cuddly armful seemed to have had a tonic effect on his temper.

With branches found in the wood, and lengths of nylon rope, he soon had a clothes line erected. Mary, waking from her nap to find Jane pegging out the tenth sock, said, "Have you done *all* the washing? You're a treasure, Jane. Can I book you for next summer?"

Jane smiled. "If they knew what a sinecure it was, you'd have half the girls at U.E.A. queueing for the post!"

The children returned from exploring. They had noticed that a gallery had been cut in the rock face behind the water-fall on the opposite side of the valley.

"Can we go over before tea, Mum?" asked John.

"Why not? Let's all go," said Mary.

Chloe Brundall had finished sunbathing, and had put on a shirt and pants when they went by her caravan. She smiled at Mary. "Going to town?"

Their objective explained, she said, "May I come with you? My parents have gone to Interlaken and may not be back for some time. I'm feeling a little lonely among all these foreigners."

To reach the far side of the valley, they walked in the direction of Lauterbrunnen. The road crossed a rushing river, the

White Lütschine, and circled a church with a six-sided, shin-gled steeple pointing to the lapis lazuli sky. Where the road twisted right, into town, Mrs. Wroxham's party turned left, first down a lane, and then up a steep, winding *fussweg* which led to the foot of the Staubbachfall.

It was cool, even a little gloomy, in the shadow of the mighty cliff. Like the flowing white tail of an Arab horse, the falling water was blown this way and that by the breeze. At present, a light west wind was blowing it down-valley so that, to reach the steps to the gallery behind the main cascade, they had to run through the equivalent of a heavy rain shower.

There was something about the cliff and the waterfall which frightened Thomas, and made his lower lip tremble. Jane of-fered to stay with him while Mary went up to the gallery, but, much as he liked her, this was one of the occasions when he felt safest holding tightly to his mother.

"I'm not eager to get soaked myself," said Mary dryly. "The rest of you go. We'll watch. Yes, you can stay here if you'd rather, darling" – to Francesca.

Led by the three older children, Jane raced through the down-pour and up the water-shiny steps cut in the rock. They were perilously slippery and she was not surprised, half way up them, to hear a shriek from behind her. Instinctively, she checked and turned, and was in time to see Chloe lurching backwards and being neatly fielded by David, who was bring-ing up the rear.

Perhaps Chloe knew from experience that being wet did not spoil her charms, but enhanced them. She took time to recover her balance, and when she and David finally reached the shelter of the gallery, they looked as if they had been acting one of those wrestling-in-the-surf film love scenes Jane thought acidly.

David's shirt was plastered to his chest and shoulders, and his wet dark face had the gleam of bronze in the half-light behind the waterfall.

Chloe was equally drenched, and her white shirt, now

almost transparent, clung to rounded shoulders and a chest as soft and bosomy as David's was hard and muscular. Jane was not dissatisfied with her own figure, but she knew that she lacked the other girl's super-femininity. Chloe had small hands and feet, and a waist which, if it did not actually measure less, looked much smaller than Jane's because of the more lavish curves above and below it.

The children were disappointed to find that looking at the valley through a waterfall was much like seeing it in the rain. Later, they learned from the camp warden that the time to visit the gallery was when the morning sun was shining on it.

Back at the camp, Mary and Jane started the supper preparations. Suddenly, although the sky was still cloudless, they found themselves sitting in shade. The sun would not set for another two hours, but it had sunk too low in the sky to reach the depths of the valley. The pinewoods and pastures on top of the cliffs were still golden. The icy ramparts of the Breithorn were tinged with mother-of-pearl pink. But the town and the camp and the long green floor of the valley were plunged in premature twilight.

"I see what David meant now. What a pity. However, one can't have everything, and this is still a lovely place," said Mary.

While the Wroxhams were eating their evening meal, campers who had been out for the day began to return from rambles, sightseeing trips, and shopping in the large resort of Interlaken, through which the Wroxhams had passed on their way to the valley.

"Look at those super boots," whispered John, as a couple of campers clumped past in buckled knee breeches, thick-knit stockings and heavy, studded leather climbing boots.

A mini-car with a French registration and the sign of an international car hire firm came bouncing up the rough drive to park by a small blue ridge tent near the Wroxhams' pitch. The driver, a young man with a Zapata moustache, was accompanied by a girl with jet-black hair sliding over her shoulders, black eyes, and a lovely patrician face.

"Where does that person come from, Mummy?" asked Emma discreetly.

"She's an Indian."

"A Red Indian? Like Pocahontas?"

"No, from India. Like Mrs. Gandhi."

"She isn't wearing an Indian dress."

"A sari wouldn't be practical for camping in that little tent. I expect she has some lovely ones in her luggage."

The young couple, noticing the newcomers, nodded and smiled. Seeing that the Wroxhams were at the fruit and coffee stage, the man strolled over and introduced himself. He was an American. He and his wife were doctors. Newly-qualified, they were breaking their journey to India, to see her family, with a summer-long camping tour of Europe.

After supper, the Wroxhams went for a leisurely walk through Lauterbrunnen. Many of the other evening strollers were wearing the massive boots admired by John. But, as his uncle pointed out, the boots displayed in the shop windows were much lighter and less impressive. Furthermore, it was obvious that most of those tourists who were dressed as if they intended to tackle the Eiger were in no condition to run up a steep flight of stairs.

"You mean they're like the people who come to the Norfolk Broads and buy yachting caps for themselves, but don't make their children wear life-jackets, like we always have to," said John.

"Precisely," said David sardonically.

The children stopped to look at a tank full of trout by the entrance to a hotel. While they were gazing, out came a tall-hatted chef with a scoop net. He unlocked the lid of the tank, deftly netted two fish, and returned indoors.

"Is he going to *cook* them?" wailed Emma, when the significance of this manoeuvre dawned on her.

"Do look at that colossal cow bell across the road," said her mother hastily. "I shouldn't have thought a cow would be able to raise its head with a bell of that size round its neck."

It was shortly after this that Jane, without pausing to think before she uttered, said, "Here comes Cuddly Chloe."

"Sorry – what did you say?" asked David, turning a keen look upon her.

She had hoped he had not heard her lapse. Luckily, Mary had not. Flushing, she answered, "Here comes Miss Brundall with her parents."

His eyes glinted, but he didn't say anything. Jane could have kicked herself for allowing her antipathy to show, even for an instant. David would never believe that it was not sour grapes about Chloe's superior attractions which made her dislike her. Belinda far outshone Chloe, and Jane had warmed to Belinda the moment they met. But there was something about Chloe which made her uneasy.

The Brundalls were an affable couple in their late fifties. After the introductions, the two parties fused and continued to stroll in pairs; David with Chloe, Mary with Chloe's mother, and Jane with her father.

On their return to the camp, Mrs. Brundall said to Mary, "Won't you come in for a drink? I think we can find room for everyone with a bit of a squeeze."

"It's kind of you, but the children were up very late last night. I think they should go to bed now."

"I'll look after them, Mrs. Wroxham," Jane volunteered.

"Well . . . if you wouldn't mind, Jane," Mary assented.

Thomas fell asleep within seconds of being tucked in. Knowing that nothing would rouse him before the morning, Jane agreed to read another chapter of *A High Wind In Jamaica* to the other children. They were enjoying this macabre novel, one of her own childhood favourites, because the five children who were the chief characters in the story were so like themselves.

Jane was in bed, catching up with some serious reading, when Mary returned to the van.

Mary surprised her by saying, "Oh, dear, *what* a boring end
110

to the evening. And now, I suppose, we shall be expected to reciprocate."

"Didn't you like them?" asked Jane, putting aside her book.

"I suppose I didn't *dis*like them. It's a matter of wavelengths. Mrs. B. is one of those women who never reads, and who condemns all foreign food without ever having tried any; and Mr. B. talks of nothing but cars. Also they showed us what seemed like two thousand snapshots of their other holidays. It was rather hard to enthuse over endless photos of Chloe posed here, there and everywhere."

Jane received the impression that Mary, too, was not keen on Chloe. But she said only, "Would it help to have an outdoor, camp fire party, and to ask the two doctors to come as well as the Brundalls? They couldn't show snaps by firelight."

"People who inflict their holiday photos on other people will do it anywhere," said Mary. "All the same, it's a very good idea. Maybe tomorrow we'll get to know some more campers, and throw a real bangers-and-beans feast."

Jane found it hard to sleep that night. In the warmth of her *schlafsack,* some insect bites on her legs had begun to itch. And although the valley was free of all man-made noises, the torrential flow of the Lütschine, and the noise from the Staubbachfall, sounded much louder at night. Indeed, by some trick of echo, the waterfall sounded as if it were pouring down the cliff on their side of the valley.

Had she had a quiet mind, she would have slept in spite of these disturbances, but her thoughts were far from peaceful. Tomorrow was Friday, the night when Mary had arranged to telephone her husband again. If Doctor Wroxham was able to fly out to join them, there might only be another forty-eight hours before David departed. Unless Chloe's advent was sufficient inducement for him to stay in the valley. Either way, whether he went or remained, it was unlikely that Jane would ever again have him all to herself, as she had on the road to the Susten Pass.

Remembering their time together on the hillside – could it

111

have been only yesterday? – she regretted bitterly her folly in dining with Willem. Now, when it was too late, she saw that from the very beginning her attitude to David had been one, not of sensible caution, but of hypocrisy and cowardice.

He had always attracted her. Merely to look at his hands was more exciting than holding hands with poor Willem. Had she had any courage, she would not have worried about being hurt, about making a fool of herself. She would have smiled instead of frowning, agreed instead of arguing, and for once in her life enjoyed the pleasures of the present, instead of reserving all life's rewards for the future.

As she listened to the church bell striking a quarter past twelve, Jane resolved that if ever she had a second chance she would behave very differently.

Both Mary and Jane slept late the following morning. When they emerged from the van, they found that David had already been to the shop for fresh bread, milk and peaches. Now he was frying sausages, tomatoes and eggs.

"Why the big breakfast?" enquired his sister.

"If it's okay with you, the children and I are going to walk up to Mürren."

"Can I go, Mummy?" asked Thomas.

Mary smiled, and stroked his round cheek. "Do you realise where Mürren is, Tomkin? Right at the very top of that great cliff, darling."

"You're not quite big enough to climb up there this year. You and I will find something much nicer to do," Jane promised him, as his face fell.

"No, no. I'll look after him today, Jane. You go to Mürren with the others. That is, if you *want* to toil up there," said Mrs. Wroxham. As they walked to the wash-house together, she confided, "I would go if my husband were here. But the truth is that, left to myself, I'm really a very slothful type. It's only to please Peter that I swim and play tennis and so on. As for plodding up and down mountains, my dear, I would much rather stay in the valley and have a nice lazy day with Thomas and Francesca."

While they were having breakfast, Chloe came by in a dressing-gown of white *broderie anglaise* threaded with pale blue ribbons. Her feet were thrust into wedge-heeled mules of quilted white nylon with blue tulle pom-poms, and her toilet bag was blue and white.

"We're going for a ramble. Care to come?" asked David, rising at her approach.

"I'd love to," Chloe said eagerly.

"You'll need walking shoes. Sandals won't do. We're going to Mürren and back."

Her enthusiasm diminished slightly. "Mürren? How far is it?"

"About three thousand feet up that cliff," he said. "You can't quite see it from here."

"*Three thousand feet!* I thought you meant walking, not climbing."

"It is a walk."

"Not my sort," Chloe said, with feeling. "I'll go to Thun with my parents. See you later, perhaps." Looking rather put out, she continued on her way to the wash-house.

"Fancy asking her to come," said John. "You can see what a dead loss she'd be."

Mary said mildly, "Don't be rude, John." David said nothing, but sat down and sipped his scalding coffee, and watched Chloe until she disappeared, his expression never less readable.

When the walking party was ready to go, Mary drove them as far as Stechelberg, a hamlet several kilometres up the valley, where the motor road came to an end.

They set out from Stechelberg at the same time as a fair-haired, bearded young man, laden with a large rucksack topped by a bedroll. After exchanging a few words with David, and mentioning that he was on his way to the Youth Hostel at Gimmelwald, he soon drew ahead of them, marching along at a brisk pace in spite of the load on his back.

"Gosh, he must be strong," remarked John. "Do you think he's a real mountaineer?"

"I doubt it," David said dryly. "He won't keep up that speed for long."

Their way, so far a gentle slope, suddenly changed to a wooded zig-zag so steep that much of it was in steps John led the way, followed by the twins, then Jane with David coming last. Presently, Jane paused and stood aside. "I think we should change places. I'm sure I'm holding you up. Won't you come in front of me?"

"Yes, I will – to slow you down. You're going at it much too fast. Have a breather, and enjoy the view. We're supposed to be doing this for pleasure, not as a punishment."

The path was near a roaring cascade. Presently, at a place where it overlooked the foaming rush of white water, they found the bearded young man having a rest. His face was scarlet and beaded with great drops of sweat. His tartan shirt was wet through. He looked exhausted.

"See?" murmured David to John, when they had passed out of his hearing. "The correct way to walk in mountain country is slowly and steadily, not hell for leather like that lad."

Higher up, where the path bridged the cascade, and notices warned walkers to be on the alert for falling boulders, they had a refreshing drink of ice-cold stream water. Then, for a little way, the path declined before it rose again. The landscape changed from tall firs with only sparse undergrowth to deciduous woodland and sunlit pastures.

David took off his shirt, and stowed it in the top of the khaki haversack containing their rations. Jane, still behind him, watched the play of muscle under his brown-silk skin and wished she had had the forethought to wear the top of her swimsuit instead of a bra, as even her cotton-knit shirt felt hot on such a glorious mountain morning.

They passed a chalet, the low-pitched, shingle-clad roof anchored against winter storms with large stones. The wooden shingles had a weathered to a lovely silvery grey shade. An old

114

man looked out of the upper window, and gave them a friendly good-day. A sledge with hand-fashioned wood runners stood by the door.

"What did he say, Uncle David?"

"He said '*Grüetzi*.' It's the Swiss form of '*Grüss Gott*' which is high German for 'Greetings!'," David explained.

"Oh, dear, I'm so puffed," Emma exclaimed rather wearily.

"We'll stop for lunch soon. I'll give you a pull." David clasped her small hand and pulled her along behind him as if she were on a ski-tow. The path here was very hard going. Jane could feel the backs of her legs beginning to ache, and Mürren, which they could see now, was still a long way above them.

They had lunch on a bench above the hamlet of Gimmel-wald where there was a cable car station.

"I'll do it. You rest," said David, when Jane would have dealt with the lunch.

Watching him cutting the loaf, buttering the slices, dividing the cheese and salami as capably as any woman, she remembered something from Mrs. Gaskell's *Cranford*, the novel she had had to study for her G.C.E.

Forgotten for years, the passage came back word for word. *He immediately and quietly assumed the man's place in the room; attended to everyone's wants, lessened the pretty maid-servant's labour by waiting on empty cups, and bread-and-butterless ladies; and yet did it all in so easy and dignified a manner, and so much as if it were a matter of course for the strong to attend to the weak, that he was a true man through-out."*

"Where *were* you?" asked Emma, making passes in front of Jane's face to rouse her from her reveries. "That's what Mummy always says when we daydream," she added explana-torily.

"I was at a card-party at Miss Matty Jenkins' house," said Jane, to the mystification of the children. She glanced at David. "Have you ever read *Cranford*?"

"Yes, but only because I once had measles at my grand-mother's home where the alternative to *Cranford* was Macaulay's *Lays of Ancient Rome*. I can't pretend to remember it. Is it a favourite of yours?"

"No, some lines came into my head in the curious way that things do suddenly come back to one."

"Yes, memory is an extraordinary faculty. You mentioned the Chevalier Bayard recently. Have you read his life story?"

The reminder of their clash in the museum – had he forgotten already where and when she had mentioned Bayard? – made her glad she was masked by sun-glasses.

She shook her head. "All I know is that he was '*le chevalier sans peur et sans reproche*' – the knight without fear or fault," she translated for the benefit of the children.

"Which makes him sound an intolerable prig, don't you think?" David said, looking at her with an absence of expression which convinced that he *did* remember how Bayard had entered the conversation originally.

"Actually, he wasn't," he went on. "Some time ago I bought a small second-hand book called 'The Loyal Servitor's Right Joyous History of the Chevalier Bayard'. He obviously deserved his reputation, but he was a long way from being a saint. In fact in the connection in which you mentioned him, he was rather the reverse."

"Really?" Jane avoided a longer reply by biting off a chewy mouthful of bread and sausage. A few seconds later everyone's attention was diverted by the sight of an orange cable-car skimming from Gimmelwald to Mürren.

"Lazy lot!" John said scornfully of the tourists inside the vehicle.

An elderly couple, coming downhill, wished them "*Guten appetit*." The woman, having passed them, glanced over her shoulder and murmured something to her husband.

"She thinks we're a nice-looking family," David translated, with a quizzical look at Jane. "Do you object to being taken for a *hausfrau* . . . my *hausfrau*?"

116

Remembering her resolution during the night, she mustered all her aplomb and managed to smile as she said, "On the contrary, I'm flattered."

His left eyebrow rose. He said dryly, "Those dark glasses give you a spurious sophistication. Without them nobody could possibly mistake you for the mother of this trio."

They finished their meal with the peaches which in the valley were cheaper than apples.

Jane thought: From now on every time I eat a peach, I shall think of today.

"Look . . . look! I think that's an eagle." John sprang to his feet, pointing excitedly. "Can I use your glasses, Uncle David?"

David handed the boy his fieldglasses. Mindful of their value – he longed for a pair of his very own – John slipped the strap over his head before he adjusted the focus. But the bird he thought he had seen had disappeared behind a crag on the far side of the valley, or perhaps he had only imagined it.

"I hope we see *one* while we're here," he said disappointedly, handing back the fieldglasses. "The Swiss eagle's called a *steinadler*. It has an eight-foot wing-span. In one of my bird books it says that they have been known to carry off chamois and even children. Not ones as big as Thomas, but little babies who can't walk yet. It also said in the book that if *steinadlers* see anyone near the edge of a cliff, they dive-bomb and scare them until they overbalance."

"What do they do that for?" asked Emma, with an apprehensive glance at the sky.

"To tear chunks out of them after they've plunged to their death," John explained, with relish.

"It sounds to me as if that bird book was written a very long time ago by someone with more imagination than knowledge," remarked David.

Not far beyond where they had lunch, the narrow path joined a wider one which sloped more gradually. The children, refreshed by their rest, began to chatter among themselves, and

117

to take short cuts by scrambling up the grassy banks between the twists and turns of the path.

David and Jane strolled in their wake. There was room to walk side by side now, but he seemed disinclined to converse.

Mürren, like Lauterbrunnen, consisted of one long main street, but differed from the town in the valley in having no motor traffic. Visitors came by the rack railway or, like the young Wroxhams, on foot. Mürren had one very large and luxurious-looking hotel, the Palace Hotel des Alpes. But it was not open in summer, only in the winter sports season.

"Anyone for an ice-cream?" asked David, as they came to the Edelweiss Café which had tables set outside in the sun.

The children had ices and fruit drinks. David and Jane had iced coffee. For Jane, who had accompanied Emma to the Damen while he and John queued at the self-service counter, he had also chosen a large slice of strawberry layer cake, filled and decorated with fresh cream frosting.

"Even if you had to worry about your figure, the climb would counterbalance however many calories there are in that," he said. "You don't dislike gooey things, do you?" – as an afterthought.

"No, I love them," she confessed.

At a shop not far from the café, the twins chose postcards to put in their holiday log book, and John bought a badge to add to those already sewn on the sleeves of his anorak. Jane, glancing in the window of a shop selling more expensive souvenirs, had her attention arrested by some carved and coloured wood figures of Swiss country people. They had something about them quite different from any of the carvings she had seen elsewhere. Clearly they were the work of an artist in wood, and not mass-produced like most of the ornaments in the shops. The smallest figures were thirteen francs. The six-inch ones were not priced. She guessed they were far beyond her means.

Aware that one of the others was coming to join her, and thinking it was John, she said, "Do look at these. Aren't they good? The faces are tiny, but so expressive."

118

"So you've finally seen something you covet? Why not buy one?" It was David who had come alongside her.

"Oh, no, I don't think I will," she said casually, turning away from them. "One doesn't need a memento of a lovely day like today."

Further on, near the station, there was a public garden with a breathtaking view of the summits of the Mönch and the Eiger. The children took turns to look through a large telescope mounted on a pedestal. David used his fieldglasses, and Jane rested her arms on the sun-warmed stone balustrade overlooking the valley, and gazed at the fearsome Eiger which had challenged so many climbers to risk their lives, often to lose them.

She thought of all the places in the world which most people knew by name, but only a few people saw. She thought how lucky she was to be here in this beautiful mountain resort, and she thought what a pity it was that, after she had graduated and begun her career, she would have only three weeks a year in which to travel. With an almost physical shock, she caught herself wondering if she had chosen the right career, and if it was too late to change to some other work with greater opportunities to see more of the world.

"Care to have a look through these?" David asked her, offering the glasses.

"Oh . . . thank you," she said absently, still reeling, mentally, from the discovery that the whole foundation of her future, which had seemed rock-firm, had begun to crumble.

David moved behind her, and lifted the strap over her head. Instinctively she put up her hands to hold the glasses. But instead of surrendering them to her, he continued to hold them.

"Is the focus right for you – or blurred?"

"A little blurred."

He made an adjustment. "Better?"

"Yes, that's fine . . . perfect, thank you."

He let her take hold of the glasses, but continued to stand behind her. For a moment or two, his left hand rested on her shoulder. "If you find them heavy to hold still, prop your elbows on the parapet," he suggested.

"Goodness, how close they bring everything," she said, in a rather stifled voice.

"They're ten-fiftys – made in Japan."

"Really?" Judging by his tone, he was no more conscious of touching her than if it was Emma's shoulder beneath his palm. Would he never move away? If she swayed by an eighth of an inch, she would find herself leaning against him. "Have you ever wanted to climb a mountain?"

"Not one as formidable as the Eiger. I suppose you wouldn't remember the first time the north face was climbed in winter? It was in 1961. Four men spent six nights and seven days struggling up to the summit."

"What an appalling time for their wives and parents. A week of constant suspense," she said, with a shiver. "I should think, by the time they came down, their wives must almost have hated them for putting them through such an agony of anxiety."

David's hand left her shoulder. He moved a little aside.

Jane lowered the glasses to look at him. "I suppose you admire men like that."

"For having more courage than I have – yes," he replied. "But I agree with you. If a man wants to dice with death, he shouldn't expect a woman and children to love and depend on him."

His answer, his seriousness, surprised her.

The children came over to them, and David glanced at his watch. "Do we walk down, or go by train?" he asked.

They voted to walk. "Going down will be easy," said Edward.

As they were retracing their way through the little town, David remembered that he wanted to cash a traveller's cheque.

"You four go on ahead. I'll soon catch you up," he said.

At first, going downhill was easy compared with coming up, and now the spectacular view which, before, they had had to pause to admire, was before their eyes all the time.

When David joined them, he said, "I've just heard something which will interest you, John. You're a James Bond fan, aren't you? This is where the film 'On Her Majesty's Secret Service' was made. I heard some people talking about it in the Change office. Have you seen the film?"

"No, not that one yet. But I've read the book. There's a terrific skiing bit in it. Fancy the film being made here!"

Their descent was by no means as easy as Edward had forecast. Where the path had been particularly hard to climb, it was almost as hard to go down. Below the difficult stretch, they rested and David distributed some bars of milk chocolate which he had bought after cashing his cheque.

The twins were decidedly droopy when the party returned to Stechelberg where Mary was waiting for them. Some time during the day she had had her hair set, but she did not look much refreshed by her leisurely day with the two youngest children.

When they were all in the van, she said, "I'm afraid there's disappointing news. I telephoned Daddy half an hour ago. He can't fly to Zürich on Sunday. He can't join us here after all." Her voice shook a little, and quickly she switched on the engine and started to drive back to camp.

It was when Jane returned from a shower that she found the wooden woman in her carrier. The carrrier, a large one of striped nylon fabric, had been given to her by Mary as the only available substitute for her stolen suitcase. The figure, wrapped in tissue paper, was lying on top of the towel in the carrier.

When Jane unwrapped it and saw the six-inch farmer's wife dressed in an apron and kerchief, her print sleeves rolled up to her elbows, her cheeks round and rosy as polished apples, she gave a soft sound of delight. Of all the carved figures in the shop window, this was the one she had liked best. How strange that he should have guessed her preference. It must have been

David who had bought it for her. It couldn't have been one of the children.

Looking out of the window, and seeing David strolling back from the wash-house with a towel slung over one shoulder, his dark hair wet from the shower, she jumped down from the van and ran across the grass to meet him.

"I've just found her. I – I don't know how to thank you. She's the one I liked best of them all."

He said, openly teasing her, "I'm glad you're happy about something, but what makes you think I'm behind whatever it is?"

"It could only be you – although I can't think why you should give me such a charming present."

His expression changed to the one she could never interpret. "A small *amende honorable*, perhaps. I was rather brutal to you yesterday."

"Oh," said Jane, oddly deflated. Somehow, during today – she couldn't say precisely when – yesterday had lost its sting. Until he reminded her of it, she had almost forgotten the Transport Museum. Lucerne seemed a long way behind them.

"Well . . . thank you very much," she repeated, in a more restrained tone. Then, as they walked back to the tent, "David, your sister must be feeling terribly downhearted. Wouldn't it be a good idea to take her out to dinner tonight? Perhaps to that place in Lauterbrunnen where we saw the trout tank? I can mind the children. That's why I'm here."

"I'll suggest it to Mary," he agreed. "It's wretched luck for them both. They're not the sort of couple who don't mind being separated."

"It's disappointing for you, too."

"I'd already decided to stay the course whether Peter joined us or not. I –"

He broke off as someone said, "Good evening. Did you have an enjoyable day?"

It was Chloe Brundall's father. A few moments after he joined them, Jane heard a small child howl in the coppice under the cliff. Thinking it might be Thomas, she left the two men chatting and went to investigate.

It was not Thomas, but his new-found friend, Gilles, who had gashed his leg on a broken branch. Accompanied by Thomas, Jane restored the little French boy, still bawling, to his parents, a friendly couple both of whom spoke excellent English.

Crossing the field once more, Jane saw that now Chloe had joined the men and was talking vivaciously to David. Was it because of Chloe that he had decided to "stay the course", as he put it?

A little later, while Jane was extracting a splinter from John's palm, his mother reappeared. She had been absent for some time and, looking at her face, Jane suspected that she had been down to the lower washroom, giving vent to her disappointment in the only place where, on a camping trip, one could be certain of privacy.

Mary said, "Jane, it was sweet of you to suggest to David that he should take me out tonight. I have a better idea. We'll do as we did at Waldshut. We'll put Tomkin to bed in the van, and give our tastebuds a treat at the inn at Stechelberg."

The entrance to the inn at Stechelberg led into a wood-panelled bar, full of people in hill-walking clothes. Beyond an inner bar-cum-snackroom, there was a large, modern dining-room with flowers and soft lights at each table. In a corner, two tables were placed together length-wise to accommodate a large party, such as Mrs. Wroxham's.

"Does everyone want to try *fondue*?" asked Mary, as a waitress presented menus to the three adults.

"Jane has tried it. What was it like, Jane?" asked Edward.

"No, I've never had *fondue*, Edward."

"I thought that's what you were going to eat when you went out with Willem at Lucerne?"

"No, we had something else," she answered.

She wondered if, in spite of his apparent concentration on the wine list, David was listening. But when he looked up from

123

the *Weinkarte* his attention did not turn on her, but on someone entering the dining-room. As he pushed back his chair and stood up, Jane knew, without looking, who had arrived, and what would happen.

Her intuition proved correct. "Hello again," said Chloe. And, when her parents had greeted Mary, Mrs. Brundall said, "May we join you?"

As there was plenty of room for them, Mary had no alternative but to welcome the suggestion. Perhaps she did. Perhaps it was only Jane's fancy that her smile was a courtesy, masking feelings more accurately reflected in John's furtive grimace at Edward as the two boys waited to sit down again.

The Wroxham children were not shy. They were used either to being left out of the grown-ups' table talk when it was beyond them, or included in topics they could discuss intelligently. They were unaccustomed to the special, simplified, artificially jolly conversation which Mr. and Mrs. Brundall addressed them. Embarrassed, they could find nothing to say but a mumbled "Yes, thank you," or "No, thank you."

Chloe, finding that David was having *fondue*, decided to be adventurous. Her parents preferred to play safe with pork chops and chips.

The *fondue* arrived in a blue earthenware *caquelon*, and the waitress carefully regulated the flame of the burner which would keep the molten cheese bubbling gently without burning. She then brought a second *caquelon* for the children, and explained that they must spear small pieces of bread on the end of long-handled forks, dip the bread in the cheese, twirl the fork, and place the cheese-coated bread between their teeth.

"You must take care your bread does not fall in the *fondue*. If that happens, the gentlemen must pay for a bottle of wine," she warned, smiling at David and John. "If the ladies drop their bread" – looking at Chloe and Jane – "they must give a kiss to each man."

Chloe giggled, and looked provocatively at David. Mary and Jane had put on clean shirts and pants, but Chloe and her mother had changed as if they were on a cruise, or staying at a smart hotel. Mrs. Brundall was wearing a matronly Lurex brocade suit, and Chloe was in violet crushed velvet pants with a matching bolero over a lavender satin shirt. She looked as strokable as a kitten, and was attracting many interested glances from the husky young climbers at the other tables.

But if Belinda was here, thought Jane, no one would look twice at Chloe. Her irrational dislike of the other girl vexed her, and her crossness with herself must have shown in her face.

"Jane . . ."

She came out of her thoughts to find David looking at her.

". . . Have you a headache?"

"No. Was I scowling? Sorry." She did not have to assume a more cheerful expression. For some seconds, the fact that he had noticed her looking gloomy had a far more happy-making effect than the wine in her glass, or the *kirsch* in the hot, spiced cheese.

"I didn't realise the Swiss went in for garlic and oil," remarked Mrs. Brundall disapprovingly, after tasting the tossed green salad accompanying her chop. "Have you been to Spain, Mrs. Wroxham? Oh, the oil they use there! Everything swims in it. I don't think we had one meal we could say we enjoyed, did we, Ronald?"

"Really? What a shame! Do you never use garlic or oil at home?" asked Mary politely.

"Good gracious, no!" Mrs. Brundall looked quite offended. "You always say that good food doesn't need to be disguised with fancy sauces, don't you, Ronald?"

"Well, I must admit that roast beef, Yorkshire pud. and spring cabbage is one of my favourite meals," said Mary. "But with a family as large as ours, roasting joints are a luxury nowadays. I don't know how I should cope without stretchable foreign dishes like spaghetti Bolognese and paella."

While this conversation was going on at one end of the table, the children were discussing among themselves possible

125

expeditions for the next day. Jane had one ear tuned to their chatter, and the other to what Chloe was telling David about her job as a receptionist at the headquarters of one of the regional television companies.

When the two families left the inn, they found that the sky had clouded. The air had a heavy stillness, suggesting rain during the night.

Prompted by a nudge from his wife, Mr. Brundall invited David and Mary to spend the rest of the evening in their caravan, but Mary declined, explaining that the mountain air had made her sleepy and she intended to have an early night. David said only that he had things to do.

As soon as they returned to the camp he began cutting, with the aid of a spare tent peg, a shallow channel all round the back of the tent, which was pitched on a slight slope. In answer to his sister's enquiry, he said, "I think there'll be a storm before morning, and I don't want to have to do this in a deluge in the small hours."

Mary and Jane were in their bunks when, after tapping on the door, he put his head inside the van to say, "I'm going for a stroll for an hour or so."

"What! After all the hiking you did today?" exclaimed his sister.

He looked at Jane. "Has our climb knocked you out?"

"No, but I can't say I feel energetic."

"Nor do I, but I don't feel like turning in yet. The kids were unconscious as soon as their heads hit the pillow. Even John didn't want to read tonight. Good night, girls. Sleep well." He withdrew.

Perhaps he's going to have a nightcap with the Brundalls after all . . . or a stroll with Chloe, thought Jane.

"I hope it isn't overcast tomorrow," Mary said drowsily. "I was thinking we might do the trip up to the Jungfraujoch. But it's rather expensive, and we don't want to spend all that money to see nothing but clouds. Don't turn out the light on my account. Read for as long as you like, my dear. A search-

126

light wouldn't keep me awake tonight."

Jane did attempt to read, but found it impossible to concentrate. Her intuition was telling her, even more strongly than before, that at this very moment David and Chloe were leaning, elbow to elbow, on the bridge across the Lütschine, and that before they returned to the camping, David would have found out whether Chloe was as cuddly as she looked.

And the real reason I dislike her is not because I sense that she's a shallow, self-centred person, but because I wish I were in her place, Jane admitted to herself, as she switched off the light and lay down.

The storm which David had forecast reached the valley soon after midnight. Surprisingly, even when the thunder and its echoes were an almost continuous boom, Thomas never stirred. But Mary and Jane sat up and drew back the curtains to watch the flashes of lightning. As the storm moved on, the rain arrived; first a violent deluge lasting two or three minutes, followed by a steadier downpour. Lights in most of the caravans and autovans, and in several tents, showed that most people staying at the Schützenbach were not only awake but probably brewing tea.

The noise of the rain beating on their roof made it impossible for Mary and Jane to hear the commotion going on inside a newly-arrived frame tent a little way down the field from their pitch. But a gas-lamp was burning inside the tent, and they could see the silhouettes of two or three people who were moving about in an agitated manner. As they watched, a tall, black-clad figure emerged from the Wroxhams' tent.

It was David, wearing an oilskin coat and leggings. By torchlight, he set to work to dig a drainage channel round the other tent.

"Oh, that's what's the matter!" Mary exclaimed, grasping the reason for the strange antics going on inside the new tent. "They're awash, poor wretches."

Next morning, Jane woke to the clanging of cowbells. A small herd was passing along the road below the camp. The leading cow was wearing one of the very large bells they had seen in the shops, but she did not appear to find its weight burdensome.

Jane had expected to ache all over, but to her surprise she was not stiff from the unaccustomed exertion of yesterday. When she returned from the wash-room, she saw David filling a bucket from a pile of chippings beside the driveway which circled the camp.

"Good morning. You had a disturbed night in spite of your precautions," she remarked.

He shrugged. "The three damsels in the new tent were in danger of floating downhill on their air-beds."

"Oh, they're damsels, are they?" she said. "That explains it."

Her reply was intended to be a joke, and she was disconcerted when David, instead of smiling, said in an unamused tone, "No doubt it's a very quaint concept to your generation, but long ago, in my formative days, your sex relied on mine to deal with certain kinds of crisis. Stupidly, I forgot to ask those three if they had been liberated. Although the recognised member of the union didn't volunteer her services, I noticed."

"I'm sorry," she said, taken aback.

At that moment two of the "damsels" emerged from their tent to survey the morning. They were women in their fifties, and one glance convinced Jane that they were either schoolmistresses or dons.

"Good morning." David left Jane, and walked across to talk to them.

At breakfast, it was decided that, the sky still being overcast, they would spend the morning exploring the shores of Lake Thun, and the afternoon looking round Interlaken. It was Saturday, and Mary wanted to top up her stock of provisions, and also to find presents for Mrs. Tharston, who was holding the domestic fort for her, and for old Mrs. Forncett who had been baby-sitting for the Wroxhams since John was in his carricot.

128

"I wonder how the Swiss achieve such fabulous geraniums?" Mary speculated when, during the morning, they stopped to admire a particularly attractive Bernese chalet, its first-floor balcony almost hidden by a profusion of pink, white and deep red flowers.

"Cows' urine is the secret, I believe," said David. "In winter they stand the pots in the gully in the floor of the byre."

Like many of the chalets they had seen, this one had carved and painted writing on the wall above the first floor windows with their neat green shutters and snowy voile curtains.

"What does the writing mean, Uncle David?" asked Emma.

He studied it for a moment or two. The letters were elaborately gothic, not easy to decipher at a glance.

"It says 'This is our abiding-place for a moment. Our true home is eternity'," he told her.

"You are clever." She slipped her hand into his, and peered at the tanned face so far above her own.

"I know," he said, making her giggle.

Watching them, Jane felt an absurd pang of envy for Emma who, no matter what, was always in his good graces. Jane was still at a loss to understand why he had responded so curtly to her lighthearted sally earlier on. It was unlike him to be short-tempered. The only explanation she could think of was that Chloe had been less co-operative than her behaviour dinner had led him to expect.

Further on, another chalet had a more elaborate legend neath its gingerbread eaves.

> *This house was built by Benedict Kirchner.*
> *As it happened of old, so it happens today,*
> *One is built up, another falls down.*
> *One thing, however, stands fast forever,*
> *God and His word pass never away.*

At Spiez, a resort on the lakeshore, they found small *schlöss* with a medieval stone keep surro

more sophisticated additions of later centuries. The garden behind the castle was bright with flowers. Urns overflowing with scarlet geraniums surmounted the stone pillars supporting a wrought iron balustrade from which there was a fine view of the town, and of the jetty where the Thunersee steamers moored. On a clear day, there would have been mountains in the background, thought Jane, as she kept Thomas company while the others toured the interior of the *schloss*.

Footsteps on the gravel walk made her glance over her shoulder. She had thought David had gone inside the castle. But, for reasons of his own, he was outside. He did not join her and the child, but strolled about on his own.

At two o'clock, as they finished their picnic lunch and prepared to return to Interlaken, it began to rain. At three, it was still wet. Having bought the foodstuffs she needed in the Migros supermarket near the station, Mary suggested postponing the other shopping to a dryer day.

On the way back to Lauterbrunnen, they passed a wedding party in a procession of carriages drawn by white-plumed horses. But the bride was hidden by a protective cover like a perambulator apron.

The Brundalls' car was not alongside their caravan when the Wroxhams returned to the camp. "I wonder where they've gone today?" said Mary.

"No idea," said David, in an uninterested tone.

But Jane suspected that he did know.

It was still raining after breakfast next morning when, having tidied the girls' "room" inside the tent, Jane stood under the entrance canopy and watched a young couple sharing an umbrella on their way to the washrooms.

As she watched them, amused and a little touched by their leisurely pace, David left the van and joined her. "Doesn't that sight weaken your determination to avoid matrimony?" he asked, with a nod in the direction of the honeymooners who clearly did not much care if it rained for a week.

It was the first unnecessary remark he had addressed to Jane

130

since yesterday morning. "I'm not determined to avoid it," she answered.

"Merely to postpone it until it suits your convenience, hm?"

Without waiting for her answer, he ducked inside the tent. He was too tall to stand comfortably under the canopy.

By noon the rain had ceased, but the sky remained cloudy. After lunch, the younger children were content to play with the other children in the camp. But John was restless and wanted to walk up to Wengen, the fashionable winter sports resort on the eastern side of the valley. Having failed to persuade either his mother or his uncle to accompany him, he began to coax Jane.

"Do you honestly feel like trudging up there on such a dull afternoon?" asked Mary when, after some hesitation, Jane had agreed to go with him. "There won't be much of a view with all this low cloud about. I shouldn't be surprised if it rains again later on."

Jane was not feeling particularly energetic. Today, she was rather stiff from the climb on Friday. But Wengen was not as high up the mountainside as Mürren had been, and she thought that another walk might cure her aches more effectively than would resting. Also, a walk with John would be more relaxing emotionally than an afternoon in the company of his uncle.

Soon after two o'clock, the pair of them set out by way of a path across the meadow behind the camping ground. This led them across the tracks of the rack and pinion railway, and as they approached the crossing-place a train was slowly coming up the hillside from Lauterbrunnen.

They paused to watch it go by, and then continued along a meadow path, past one or two chalets, to a dark and rather gloomy stretch of woodland with a stream cascading through it.

It was here that John glanced over his shoulder and said, in a pleased tone, "Here comes Uncle David. He must have changed his mind."

Jane, looking back, was astonished. She had assumed that

David had his own plans for the afternoon. He had spent much of the morning laying more chippings, and some sacks he had found, on the sodden grass in the tent belonging to his three damsels. As they had not had sufficient experience of tenting to bring a plastic ground sheet with them, their living conditions would have been very unpleasant without his efforts to make them more comfortable.

"Mind if I join you?" he asked, when he caught up.

"You're welcome," Jane said politely.

The path to Wengen was wider and much less steep than the way up to Mürren, but it was still fairly stiff going. Eventually, they came to a signposted fork. One arm pointed the way to the *bahnhof*, the other to the *kirche*. When Jane and David decided to take the church fork, John wanted to go the station way on his own, and to meet them in the village.

"All right, we'll rendezvous at the church," his uncle agreed.

"Will he be all right?" said Jane uncertainly, as the boy set off.

"He's ten, not two. What do you imagine could happen to him? Or is it that you don't fancy walking *à deux*?"

"What a curious idea," she said lightly.

"No more curious than some of yours."

Their path had begun to be steep, and Jane went forward at a spanking pace until David grasped her by the hand, saying, "Much too fast. Slow down, girl."

"Sorry – I forgot. You'd better lead." She halted, and stepped aside so that he could pass her.

There was not enough space on this path to allow two people to walk abreast. But probably, if there had been, he would have released her hand just as quickly, she thought regretfully.

Below the church they crossed the railway again. The backs of Jane's knees were aching severely by now. She was thankful to sink on to a bench in front of the church. She agreed with David that it was disappointing not to be able to see across the valley to Mürren, but the immediate scene of scattered chalets and undulating meadows had a peaceful charm, even on a grey day.

"John is taking a long time to get here," she said, about five minutes later.

"I expect he's dawdling through the village. Let's go and find him, shall we?"

"We said we would meet him here. We may miss him if we don't wait."

"Wengen has only one main street," David assured her. "We can't possibly miss him."

But they walked the full length of the street, and reached the station at the other end, without seeing any sign of John.

"Damn the boy! Where has he got to?" David exclaimed. "I wonder if he's in that large building over there. It sounds as if there's an ice hockey match going on. You stay here. I'll see if he's there."

"We had better go back to the church where we told him we'd be," said Jane, when he returned to her, alone. "Oh, poor little John. What can have happened to him?"

"I'll give him 'poor little John' when he does turn up," said David curtly. "You're tired. Go and have tea in the restaurant we passed. I'll find the wretched child."

"No, no – I'd rather come with you."

They returned to the church. No John. They walked back to the station. No John.

"Where *can* he be?" Jane was now really worried. "I had a feeling something would happen when we separated from him."

"Look, you're obviously exhausted. Have a rest and a snack in the café. It isn't in the least necessary for both of us to hunt for the little pest," said David, his grey eyes stony with controlled exasperation.

"Yes, and when you find him you'll lose your temper and wallop him," she said distressfully. "He'll be upset enough already. Don't you think he'll be scared at not being able to find *us*?"

"I hope he is," retorted David. "It may teach him a modi-

133

cum of sense. This isn't Zürich or Berne. He can't get run over here. I'd leave him to find his own way back. A boy of ten is not a baby."

"Oh, how can you be so unimaginative? Ten isn't very old, and this isn't an English village where he could speak to people ... ask if anyone had seen us." Fatigue and anxiety made her voice shake, her eyes blur.

Turning from him, blinking back foolish tears, she saw a small, red-faced figure hurrying wearily towards them.

The first joyous surge of relief was followed by concern about David's reaction. Turning to him, she begged, "Please ... don't be furious. Don't hit him."

He was watching the boy as she spoke. Slowly, he looked down at her, his jaw muscles taut. "I know you've never had a high opinion of my character. I didn't realise you also took me for a bully."

He swung on his heel and strode in the direction of the station.

CHAPTER V

"WHERE is Uncle David going?" asked John, as he reached her.

"He . . . I don't know . . . I expect he'll be back in a minute. What happened to you? We've been worried."

John's explanation was confused by his efforts not to cry. Half way through his muddled account of what had happened, he had to stop and clench his teeth.

"Never mind now. Explain later. The important thing is that you've found us," Jane told him huskily. With an arm round his shoulders, she steered him to the recessed doorway of a closed shop where they could pretend to be looking at something in the window display while he recovered himself.

Her sympathy, in place of the crossness he had expected, was too much for John's self-control. His flushed face crumpled, and tears squeezed from his closed eyes and trickled down his hot cheeks.

"Oh, John," muttered Jane, in a choked voice. She hugged him to her with one arm, searched for a handkerchief with the other, and shed a few tears of her own on the top of his tousled fair head.

They were still in the doorway when David came back. "There's a train going down to Lauterbrunnen in forty minutes, which gives us plenty of time for tea at the Bernerhof."

Jane, who had had a sinking conviction that he was not coming back, was inexpressibly relieved to see him. "David, I'm sorry –" she began.

"Forget it," he cut in quietly. But his face had a cold, masked look she had never seen before.

It had begun to drizzle, and the veranda tables outside the

Bernerhof were empty. Inside, one or two tables were occupied by people playing cards, and most of the others were taken by visitors who were compensating themselves for the disappointing weather with rich Swiss pastries.

David conferred with the waitress without consulting his companions. "I should take off your anorak, old chap," he advised his still-heated nephew.

John did as he suggested, and then embarked on a rather more coherent explanation of why he had been missing for almost an hour. After parting from them at the fork, he had climbed to what he thought was the village but had seen no sign of the church. Another signpost, with pointers in many directions, had been no help as by then he had forgotten the word meaning church. He had decided to double back to the first fork and follow the path taken by Jane and his uncle.

"Do you know what the word church is now?" David enquired sardonically.

"Yes – *kirche*. I'm awfully sorry, Uncle David."

"Jane was the one who was worried about you." David rose from the table and walked to one of the two wooden partitions on either side of the entrance. Watching him, Jane saw that the edge of the partition was pierced by a row of round openings, each one with a handle sticking from it. Taking hold of one of these handles, David withdrew a length of wood like a long, slender rolling pin, round which was wrapped a newspaper.

"You don't mind if I catch up with the news, I hope?" he said politely to Jane, when he returned to his seat.

"No, of course not."

"How did you know those things held papers?" asked John.

"I've seen them before." His uncle opened the paper and disappeared behind it until the waitress brought coffee for Jane, coke for John, beer for David, and a selection of cakes. Finally, she placed a small glass of amber liquid on the table beside Jane's coffee cup.

"What is this?" Jane asked David.

136

"Cognac. You may not like it, but it will make you feel better." He drank some beer, and retired behind the paper again.

Jane drank the cognac quickly, as if it were medicine. She felt its warmth coursing through her. But the only thing which could make her feel better was for David to stop being courteously distant towards her.

On the way to the station, David paused to look at something in a shop window, and John seized the opportunity to whisper, "He *is* angry with me, isn't he? – Even though he hasn't said much. Will he tell Mum, d'you think?"

"He isn't angry with you, John," she answered unguardedly.

"You mean he's angry with *you*? What about?" asked the boy, with unexpected shrewdness.

She pretended not to have heard, and a moment later David was alongside.

Like Mürren, Wengen was free of motor traffic apart from the motorised luggage trolleys being driven to and from the cuckoo clock station by liveried hotel porters.

While they were waiting for the train to come down from Wengernalp, higher up the mountain, John looked at the postcard displays, and David strolled up and down the platform. Jane watched him, her eyes troubled. Was what she had said so unforgivable? He had seemed so furious with John, and even parents had been known to shake or spank children who had caused them deep anxiety.

When they returned to the camp, Mary was entertaining an American couple who had arrived by autovan from Sierre, on the fringe of French-speaking Switzerland. So nothing was said about what had happened at Wengen.

Later, when Emma and Francesca were sharing a shower, and Mary and Jane were waiting their turn, Mary said, "I hear you had a spot of trouble this afternoon? John seems to think that, while he was missing, you and David had a quarrel about something."

"It wasn't a quarrel," Jane answered. On impulse, she told Mary everything. "It was a stupid thing for me to say. Of

137

course he wouldn't have hit John. But I was tired and up-set..." ,

"I shouldn't think *that* is what annoyed him," said Mary thoughtfully. "He probably would have cuffed John if you hadn't been there to restrain him. Peter isn't a violent man, but he wallops the children occasionally. I think they prefer one short sharp whack from him to a long nag from me. Perhaps what annoyed David was –"

She stopped short as the two little girls emerged from the shower cubicle. "You go next, Jane. I want to make sure these two are drying between their toes properly. It's so easy to pick up athlete's foot, and so hard to lose it."

Under the cascade of hot water, Jane wondered what Mary had intended to say. But by the time she came out of the shower, Mrs. Wroxham seemed to have forgotten their inter-rupted conversation.

They had dinner at the inn at Stechelberg, and sampled *rösti*, a delicious presentation of potatoes, with their minced veal with cream. Afterwards, in the car park, they encountered the Brundalls who had spent the day at Berne.

"But it wasn't much fun there on a Sunday," said Chloe moodily. "This miserable weather spoils everything. Have you been to the Casino at Interlaken yet?" – to David.

"Not yet."

Jane, being addressed by Mr. Brundall, did not hear the rest of their conversation.

There was mist in the valley early next morning, but by breakfast time it had cleared. Mary suggested going to see the Trümmelbach Falls, which they passed each time they went to Stechelberg.

This waterfall was not visible from the road like the Staub-bachfall opposite the camp. It fell through a fissure within the rock face. To see it, they had to enter a lift which took them from the foot of the cliff to a lamplit gallery thunderous with the sound of falling water. Roaring and boiling its way through the cleft in the mountainside, the Trümmelbach was

138

an impressive sight. But Jane could not help being pre-occupied with wondering whether David was still angry with her, and if, later in the day, there might be an opportunity to talk to Mary privately and resume their conversation in the washroom.

After an early lunch in camp, they set off to explore Inter-laken. It was from the Höhe Weg, the town's tree-lined central promenade flanked on one side by luxury hotels and on the other by a park, that they saw, at last, the magnificent peak of the Jungfrau.

"What does Jungfrau mean, Uncle David?" asked Edward.

"It means an unmarried girl, a maiden," he answered.

Jane, standing nearby, was reminded of their row in the Transport Museum, and of the last thing he had said to her. She looked sideways at his dark, arrogant profile. At the same instant, David glanced in her direction. Their eyes met. His face was without expression, but she could have sworn that the same recollection was in his mind.

Presently, returning along the hotel side of the Höhe Weg, they passed the entrance to the Kursaal, the casino which Chloe had mentioned the night before. Like Lucerne, Inter-laken had plenty of watchmakers and jewellers, but an equal number of shops were devoted to the sale of woodcarvings. There were carvings of bears and chamois, of world-famous statesmen and prune-wrinkled old peasant women, of alpine guides and accordion players. As well as carvings, there was an immense variety of useful objects such as salad bowls, nap-kin rings, book-ends, lamp bases, candlesticks and butter moulds.

"Interlaken must be a treen collector's paradise," said Mary as, accompanied by Jane, she left the shop where she had bought a carved container for knitting needles for Mrs. Forn-cett. "A lot of this stuff" – waving a hand at the shop windows – "is horribly vulgar and shoddy, but some of it is very nice indeed."

Jane murmured agreement. None of the carvings she had

seen could compare with the little wooden women David had bought for her in Mürren. Perhaps now he regretted that generous impulse.

He and the children were some way ahead of the two women and, unable to resist the chance to satisfy her curiosity, she said, "Mary, what were you going to say in the washroom last night? – About the real reason why David might have been put out?" she added, as Mrs. Wroxham looked rather blankly at her.

Mary hesitated. "Do you know, I can't remember. My memory becomes worse and worse. Must be old age creeping on," she said, with a laugh.

Jane bit her lip. She was positive that Mary did remember her theory, but had thought better of expressing it.

"Anyway, whatever the cause may have been, I'm sure he has forgotten all about it by now," Mary continued. "David was never the sulky type, even as a schoolboy. He has what my husband calls a low threshold of exasperation over certain things, but in general he's very even-tempered."

They had left the van in the car-park of the Migros supermarket, and Mary was locking her souvenir packages in the glove box before going to do some food shopping, when a woman strolled past, checked her pace, and turned back, exclaiming, "Mary . . . it is Mary Carleton, isn't it?"

For some seconds they gazed at each other, until Mary said, "Fanny Docking!"

"Fanny Bedingfield now. But one always remembers school friends by their original surnames. I can't think what your married name is."

"Wroxham. But, Fanny, the last time I was coerced into attending an old girls' reunion, I heard you were living in America. How come you're holidaying in Switzerland? Has your husband made a million or something?"

Fanny Bedingfield grinned. She was a freckled, Junoesque redhead with lovely teeth. She looked about seven months pregnant. "No such luck. We're not holidaymakers. We live

140

here." She looked at Jane. "Never tell me this is your daughter? My eldest is twelve, and you can't have had that much start on me."

"No, Jane is my holiday *aide*. The others – my brother and the children – must be somewhere inside the supermarket," Mary explained. "We're staying at a camping site at Lauterbrunnen."

"Well, finish your shopping and come and have drinks at our place. My kids will welcome your lot with open arms. My husband is up in the mountains somewhere, and life without father is less fun."

"You're telling me!"

Mary explained why her husband was also absent.

The shopping completed, and David and the children introduced, they set off in convoy, Fanny leading the way in her Mercedes soft-top.

"Papa Bedingfield may not have made a million, but he can't be short of a shilling if that's the family jalopy," remarked Mary. "Fanny was one of my two best friends at school," she told Jane. "But she's the world's most hopeless correspondent, and it was impossible to keep in touch. It must be fifteen years since we've met."

To her delight, the Bedingfields' home was a pinewood *schali* just like the ones they had admired from the road. "Oh, good, now we shall find out what they're like inside," she said, as David stopped the van behind her friend's car.

The arrival of the two vehicles brought three small boys pelting down the staircase from the balcony surrounding the first floor of the chalet. Fanny introduced them as Daniel, Marcus and Jacob. She then instructed all eight children to skedaddle and leave their elders in peace. "Don't worry. The two tots won't come to any harm," she said, when Jane would have gone with the little ones.

Leading the way up to the balcony, she explained that the house was not theirs, but was rented for a year. "In case Jake changes his mind about settling in Switzerland permanently.

141

At the moment we all love it here."

"What does your husband do, Mrs. Bedingfield?" David asked her.

"Call me Fanny. Jake makes films for TV. He's not attached to a corporation like the BBC, or CBS in the States. He makes the films off his own bat, and sells them to the big companies. David, as he isn't here, would you take care of the drinks, please? You know what Mary and Jane like. I'll have dry ginger on ice, please. No gin because of Jemima here" – patting her tummy. "You'll find the liquor in the big cupboard in the corner. There's a cupboard made from the wood of the arven tree in most chalets," she explained, as Mary and Jane looked admiringly round the large, wood-lined living-room, fragrant with the smell of beeswax.

The piece of furniture which Mary admired most was a pale golden dresser displaying a collection of painted plates, each one different.

"The dresser is modern, but the plates with the mottoes are antiques," said Fanny. "Jake reads German, but I don't, so I can't tell you what all the mottoes mean."

"My brother can. David, what does *wei treue Herzen ein Leben* mean?" asked Mary.

"Two true hearts for life." He came across the room, a glass in each hand, and paused to look over Jane's shoulder at the plate which Fanny had given her to examine. "*Mein ganzes Leben sei dir ergeben,*" he read. "My whole life is surrendered to you."

His voice saying those words close to her ear sent a curious sensation through Jane, an inward tremor so strong that it surprised her that her hands did not tremble.

"Isn't that a pretty sentiment?" said Fanny. "The Swiss are less phlegmatic and more romantic than they appear. Like the English."

After they had been chatting for some time, she said, "I have a brainwave. Why don't you spend the night here? We have three spare rooms. There's plenty of room for everyone.

You can telephone your camp and tell them you'll be away overnight. Do say yes, Mary. We can't possibly catch up our gossip in a mere couple of hours. Besides, I want you to have breakfast on the balcony. On a sunny morning, it's heavenly."

"Jane and Thomas and I sleep in the van anyway. If you really have room for David and the other children . . ."

"Indeed we do. That's settled, then. I'll go and tell Edith to stretch the supper a bit. Don't worry: she won't faint or give notice. She's used to unexpected guests. If you come with me, David, I'll show you the telephone."

He said, "If you wouldn't mind, Fanny, I'd like to amend your suggestion."

"By all means. What have you in mind?"

"As you and Mary will be talking your heads off, I'm sure you won't notice my absence. I've heard of a very good restaurant, and there's a girl I should like to take there – if she wants to have dinner with me."

"If she doesn't, she must be an odd one," Fanny said, laughing. "Why did I never discover you had an older brother, Mary? What a flutter in the fifth form David would have caused. Where was he then?"

Jane listened to her banter with spirits suddenly at zero.

She heard David say, "Do you think there's any hope of hiring a car in Interlaken? A travelling van is somewhat cumbersome for an evening out."

"No need to hire a car. Borrow my runabout. It's an ideal car for fond farewells," said Fanny, with an impish grin. "That is what you had in mind, I imagine?"

David gave her one of his quizzical looks. "It's always a possibility," he agreed.

Mary said, "You don't mean the Mercedes, do you? Oh, Fanny – supposing he crashed it?"

"Why should he? I expect it will be safer with him than with me, and the insurance will cover him." Fanny fished in her bag and held out her car key.

Before he took it, David said, "Thank you, but first I'd bet-

143

ter find out what the girl has to say, don't you think?" He turned. "Would you care to dine with me at Brienz, Jane?"

"M-me?" she stammered incredulously.

"Who else?"

She drew a deep breath. "I should like it very much."

"In that case you'll want to have a bath," said Fanny briskly.

Ten minutes later, lying in warm, scented water in the bathroom adjoining her hostess's bedroom, Jane still felt she was dreaming. She had been convinced that David had meant to dine with Chloe and, afterwards, take her to the casino. But if, for reasons Jane could not fathom, he preferred her company tonight, what did his motives matter?

She had asked the gods for another chance to play the light-hearted love game, and for once the gods had been indulgent. Tomorrow was the first day of September, and soon she would have to buckle down to another long winter of hard work. But tonight she need think of nothing but enjoying herself with a man who, as Fanny had said, any girl would welcome as an escort.

"I've pressed your *dirndl* for you, Jane," said Mary, coming into her friend's bedroom while Jane was combing her hair.

"Oh, how kind of you. Thank you."

"Isn't it odd?" mused Mary. "Fanny and I haven't seen each other for aeons, and yet we've picked up the threads immediately. What a chancy business life is! If we'd been five minutes earlier or later at the car park, we might never have met each other again."

"Yes," said Jane. "It is strange." She wondered if Mary had been equally startled by her brother's choice of a dinner date, and if she approved of it. Perhaps, taken up with meeting Fanny, she hadn't yet given it a thought.

The expensive interior of the Mercedes was in marked contrast to the utilitarian fittings in the travelling van. It felt strange, too, to be seated so low on the road, instead of perched up rather high. As Jane drew in her legs, and settled her shoulders against the soft leather upholstery, David closed the pas-

144

senger door and walked round the bonnet to take his place at the wheel.

"Have you driven one of these before?" she asked, as he set the car in motion as easily as if it were the van.

"Yes, once or twice," he replied.

They had passed through Brienz on their way from Lucerne to Lauterbrunnen. To return there, they had to drive through Interlaken and out of town by the road which skirted Lake Brienz. As the Mercedes purred smoothly along the busy Höhe Weg, Jane saw a young girl stare at the beautiful car, and its driver and passenger. She probably thinks this is my life style, Jane thought wryly. Little does she know!

"Perhaps we'll come back here and dance," said David, with a glance at the lighted façades of the great hotels. "We can stay out as late as we like. Mary and her chum will be chattering into the small hours, I should imagine."

"Yes, I'm glad something nice has happened for Mary."

"Why did you look so startled when I asked you to spend the evening with me?" he asked, as they left the town behind.

"I thought you were planning a date with Chloe Brundall."

David made no remark for a moment or two. Then he said, "You're not very observant, are you? There are two insuperable obstacles to a close relationship between Chloe and myself."

"Are there? What?" she asked perplexedly.

"I like garlic, and Chloe likes cigarettes." He changed down to take a tight bend. "I'm not joking. Garlic-lovers and garlic-haters are incompatible at the most fundamental level, whatever else they may have in common. The same goes for non-smokers and smokers. I'm surprised you haven't discovered that for yourself."

Jane said nothing. So he was remembering Fanny's joke about fond farewells, and David's response – *It's always a possibility*. At the time she had thought he was thinking about kissing Chloe. Now she knew that he had been thinking about her. She shivered, but not with cold, and determinedly

145

closed her mind to how the evening might end.

It was only ten miles to Brienz, a lakeside resort and wood-carving centre. The restaurant where David had booked a table was small, quiet and, she judged, extremely expensive. With the exception of one foursome, all the other diners were couples so hypnotically engrossed in each other that Lucullan food seemed wasted on them.

It was not wasted on Jane and David. They ate lake trout with lemon butter, calves' liver cooked with bacon and basil in wine, and finally a vanilla soufflé. It was the first time Jane had ever had such a meal, and she enjoyed every mouthful. But it was not until they were having coffee that she realised how skilfully David had steered the conversation past topics which might have generated tension. She could not have spent a more relaxed and comfortable hour if it had been Doctor Wroxham on the opposite side of the table.

But with the waiter no longer keeping such an attentive eye on them, and the snowy cloth cleared of everything but cups of black coffee and glasses of Benedictine, this restful rapport came to an end.

"Mary no longer has to lecture you about protecting your hands, I notice," David said suddenly, taking her right hand in his. She had been idly tracing the pattern on the rim of the unused glass ash-tray.

He stroked his thumb across her knuckles. "Have you taken my warning to heart?"

She managed to convert a sharp intake of breath into a laugh. "Perhaps."

Without taking his eyes from her face, he lifted her hand and pressed her fingers against his lips. "My technique is not up to Continental standards, I'm afraid, but I didn't start in short trousers." He replaced her hand on the table, but without releasing it.

Jane found his technique shatteringly effective. Was this his standard procedure? she wondered – To lull a girl into a false sense of easy companionship, and then without warning to

146

switch on the full force of his masculinity.

All at once she was acutely conscious that although his clasp was gentle, if he chose, those long brown fingers could make it impossible for her to disengage hers.

She said lightly, "On the contrary, I think you do it very well. I should probably be in no end of a flutter if you hadn't already explained the real reason why I'm here."

He lifted an eyebrow. "The real reason?"

"My liking for garlic."

His mouth quirked. "*One* of the reasons. There are several others I didn't mention." His fingers moved to her wrist. "Your pulse does seem a little rapid." Before she could deny it, he added, "It's getting rather close in here, don't you think? Let's go and make the most of the moonlight, shall we?" He turned away to catch the waiter's eye.

Watching him check and pay the bill, Jane wondered what he meant by "making the most of the moonlight." For the first time it occurred to her to wonder if David was one of those men who considered that wining and dining a girl entitled them to more than a few goodnight kisses.

She remembered that Belinda had once said, "They all go as far as one lets them. The difference between the lambs and the louts if that if you say 'Stop' – and you really mean it! – the lambs do, and it doesn't put them off you. The louts either pretend to be deaf, or sulk. They don't make any more dates with you. But it's no use being disillusioned if some super man makes a pass. It's the nature of the beast – even the nice beasts. Their reaction when you call a halt is the crucial thing."

Recalling this piece of worldly wisdom, Jane quailed. Her idea of a romantic evening did not include that sort of finale. She was willing – eager! – to be kissed, but she shrank from the possibility of having, in Belinda's phrase, to call a halt, however equably David might take the rebuff.

When the waiter brought David's change, he brought also a miniature black bear of Berne.

"A souvenir for the young lady," he said, in English. "Most

147

of the bears which you will see in the shops during your holiday are made here in Brienz."

Outside the restaurant they could hear the distant roar of the Giessbachfall in the forest on the far side of the lake. The main street ran alongside the lake shore. In the moonlight, the surface of the water was like black glass reflecting the glimmering peaks.

But there were many other people enjoying the lovely night and, after strolling about for a time, David said, "Let's find somewhere where we can commune with the mountains more peacefully, shall we?"

She never knew where it was that he took her. Her heart was beating too fast for her to pay attention to the route which led to a ruined belvedere built long ago on the crest of a headland. Here, there were no other people. They were high enough to see, in the distance, the golden haze which was Interlaken. David parked the Mercedes among a group of pines, and came round to open Jane's door. When he had helped her out, he reached into the back of the car and brought out a fringed silk shawl lined with cashmere.

"I borrowed this from Mrs. Bedingfield in case you were cold." He draped it over her shoulders, and slid his hands down her arms. They lingered briely above her elbows. Then he let her go.

Several wooden benches suggested that during the day the place was less lonely.

"We haven't had such a fine night since we stayed at the camp near Freudenstadt and went up the tower," he remarked, as they sat down on a bench.

"No," agreed Jane, her throat tight. She played with the fringes of the shawl, conscious that he had turned towards her, and that his arm was resting along the back of the seat. She wasn't sure whether he was looking at her, or past her to the gleaming mountains.

"That night you were confident that I wouldn't kiss you. I think tonight you're less confident, but also less averse to 'that

148

contingency', as you called it."

She said huskily, "Freudenstadt was a long time ago . . . or seems a long time ago."

He said, with amusement in his voice, "You've certainly become much more adept at parrying remarks which used to make you put on your militant expression."

"Or it could be that you've become less reactionary," she suggested.

David gave a soft laugh. She had felt him touching her hair, but had not realised that, working as delicately as a safe-breaker, he was unfastening the dark blue go-go beads which secured it. Suddenly her hair was loose on her shoulders.

It was at that instant that they heard the cars racing crazily fast up the road which led only to the belvedere. Moments later, their bench was caught in the blaze of two pairs of head-lights.

What David expected to happen, Jane wasn't sure. But possibly something unpleasant, judging by the way he sprang to his feet and stood between her and the blinding lights. She heard car doors opening, and a confusion of young, excited voices speaking Schwyzerdütsch or German.

Then David's voice, crisply authoritative, rang out and stilled the hubbub with a couple of sentences which sounded like orders.

At once the headlamps were douched, and the voices became subdued. A girl giggled, and a young man said something which sounded like an apology.

When David spoke again, he sounded relaxed and friendly. Her eyes reaccustomed to the moonlight, Jane saw that a dozen or more young people had disentangled themselves from the interiors of the two cars. Some of them were busily unpacking gear from the boots. A girl, or maybe it was a long-haired boy, began to strum a guitar.

"They're going to have a midnight cook-out. I think they're students. We are invited to join them. Would you like to stay?" David asked.

"I think we might cramp their style," she answered.

He said something in an undertone. It sounded like, "Not half as much as they've cramped mine, confound them!" but she could not be certain.

Good-humoured goodbyes, and one or two remarks which Jane suspected of being mildly ribald regrets for having broken up a party for two, followed them on their way to the Mercedes.

"What did you think might happen when they first arrived?" she asked, on the way down the hillside.

"I forgot, for a minute, which country we were in. There are places where gangs of young hooligans get a kick out of terrorising courting couples."

"Really? How beastly," she said, visualising how helpless even a man like David would have been if those young men on the hill had been toughs.

They returned to Interlaken where, for an hour or so, they joined the throng of strolling, window-shopping tourists in the streets. Then he took her to a hotel which had a night club open to non-residents and they spent another hour there. At half past twelve, they drove back to the Bedingfields' chalet where lights were still burning in the living-room.

As David switched off the engine and pocketed the key, Jane said, "It's been a wonderful evening, David. I shall never forget that delicious dinner. Thank you very much for giving me such a good time."

"*Ganz meinerseits.*"

"What does that mean?"

"The pleasure is mine."

"Oh." He seemed in no hurry to leave the car, and she wasn't sure if she should make a move to do so. Perhaps to stay still was to seem too willing to be kissed.

"I have your hair thing. Hold still." He gathered her hair together, and replaced the fastening.

It would have been so simple, when he had done it, to let his right arm slip behind her shoulders and, with his left hand, to turn her face towards his. Instead he opened the offside door and swung his tall frame out of the car. A moment later he had her door open, and was offering his hand to help her out.

As she preceded him up the outside staircase to the lantern-lit balcony, Jane couldn't believe that, after what had so nearly happened up at the belvedere, he was not going to kiss her goodnight.

"Hello, you two. Did you have a good time?" asked Mary, emerging from the living-room. Without waiting for an answer, she added, "Fanny went to bed some time ago. I've been sitting up to finish a letter to Peter. There's a vacuum flask of coffee on the table for you, and some sandwiches. See you at breakfast. Goodnight."

When she had gone, Jane said, "If Mrs. Bedingfield wants us all to have breakfast on the balcony tomorrow, I think I should turn in too. I'm not so used to late nights now."

"Sure you won't have a cup of coffee?" asked David, strolling across the room to the table where a tray had been left for them.

If he really wanted her to linger, he could have sounded more persuasive than that, Jane felt sure.

"No, I don't think I will. Goodnight – and thank you again."

"See you at sunrise. Sleep tight." He might have been smiling goodnight to Emma.

Bewildered and disappointed, Jane left the room and made her way to the small single bedroom which Fanny had insisted she must use. They were all sleeping indoors tonight, except David who was using the van.

Jane had no way of knowing how late he stayed up. It was a long time before she slept. No sooner was she in bed than she began to regret that she had not stayed downstairs a little longer, even though she had never felt less interest in food.

Lying in the carved wooden bed, under a weightlessly warm *steppdecke* which made her feel like a chicken tucked under the wing of a broody hen, she re-lived every detail of the evening. He *had* meant to kiss her, she was certain of it. But at some point in the latter part of the evening, he had changed his mind.

Why?

CHAPTER VI

To have breakfast, on a blue and gold morning, on the balcony of the Bedingfields' *schali* was, as Fanny had promised, a heavenly experience. The children sat round a long table, the four grown-ups at a smaller one. Both tables were covered with crisply starched, checked gingham cloths. The rolls were warm from the bakery, the milk was fresh from a fluffy-eared Swiss cow belonging to a neighbouring chalet-owner, who had also provided the butter, and the black cherry jam had been made by Edith, the Bedingfields' Swiss cook-housekeeper.

From where Jane was sitting, in a comfortably cushioned cane chair, she could see the summit of the Jungfrau above a clustered mass of scarlet geraniums.

"This would have been a good day for your trip to the Jungfraujoch," said Fanny to Mary. "But I'm afraid there isn't time for you to catch either of the two early morning trains which are much cheaper than the later ones. Never mind, I feel we're going to have a spell of fine weather now, although mountain weather is always terribly unpredictable."

"Where would you recommend us to go today?" asked Mary.

"That's easy. To Kandersteg, and from there by chair-lift up to Lake Oeschinen. It's one of our favourite places."

"Would your boys like to come with us? There's room for them in the van. You, too, Fanny, if you're not busy."

"I'm becoming too barrel-shaped to fit into a chair-lift," answered Fanny, laughing. "And I have some appointments today anyway. But I know the boys would love to come. You must all have dinner here tonight. Jake will be home, and will want to meet you."

To reach Kandersteg, they had to skirt Lake Thun by the road to Spiez where they had visited the *schloss*. This time there was no mist, and the Thunersee and the mountains surrounding it could be seen in their full beauty. Mary drove, David had Thomas on his lap, and everyone sang the Wroxhams' favourite going-along song, Four Wheels On My Waggon.

Jane joined in with a cheerfulness which was not assumed. While she was dressing that morning she had come to the conclusion that it was better to have been disappointed than disillusioned. Whatever Belinda might say about the nature of the beast, Jane knew that her opinion of David would have plummeted if a goodnight embrace had degenerated into a humiliating tussle. She could understand people's emotions being hard to control when they were wildly in love, but she felt it would be impossible to respect a man who was capable of making love to a girl without having any affection at all for her.

At Spiez, they turned south into the valley of the Kander. Daniel, Fanny's eldest son, was an excellent guide, and pointed out all the sights; the three identical snow-peaks of the Blümlisalp, the glittering ice-fields of the Balmhorn and the Altels, and the ruins of the Tellenburg.

"Another day you must go to see Blausee, the Blue Lake," he told them, indicating a passing signboard. "There's a trout farm there, and the water is the bluest we've ever seen."

At Kandersteg village, they parked the van in the yard below the *sesselbahn*. John and the twins gasped with excitement when they saw the two-seater chair hoists gliding down the hillside to disappear inside the station house.

While David bought the tickets, Mary divided the party into pairs.

"John with Daniel, Marcus with Edward and Jacob with Emma," she directed. "Francesca, you can go with Uncle

154

David. Thomas will come with me. That leaves you on your ownio, Jane. Do you mind? You don't suffer from vertigo, do you?"

Jane shook her head. Her dislike of heights was not severe enough to be called vertigo, but she could not help feeling a qualm as she realised that the chairs were suspended about twenty feet above the ground, less in some places and more in others, depending on the angle of the mountainside.

In the event, she did not travel alone, but with a member of another large party of tourists. There was one rather unpleasant moment when, immediately after the chair emerged from the station-house, it gave a sideways lurch. But otherwise the motion was a slow glide, like that of an escalator, and the chairs did not swing about unless their occupants made them, which a notice on the safety-bar warned them not to do. By the time she had been in mid-air for a full minute, Jane had decided that travelling by chair hoist was as heavenly as breakfasting on Fanny's balcony. The effortless soar through the bright, pure air was like being a bird.

From the topmost station, they followed a path across alpine meadows where a herd of cows strolled about, munching and eyeing the tourists. Jane, for whom, hitherto, the sound of summer had been the clop of tennis balls, felt that from now on the scent of hot grass would be linked in her mind with the gentle clonking of Swiss cowbells.

"Were you apprehensive?" asked David, falling into step with her at the rear of the party.

"About the chair hoist? I enjoyed it. I could glide up and down all day."

"Not about the hoist – about your companion. A somewhat lecherous-looking character, didn't you think?"

"Was he? I didn't take much notice of him."

"He noticed you," David said dryly.

"If you thought he was likely to . . . to pinch me, or something, it would have been chivalrous to change places."

"Cut off from the world in a chair hoist, I might have been

155

tempted to pinch you, or something, myself."

"I meant to change places with *me*," she answered, colouring. And then, before she could stop herself, she added, "You resisted the temptation last night."

His hand on her shoulder brought her to a halt, and turned her towards him. "Did you hope I would succumb?" His eyes were brilliant with amusement.

Jane's blush deepened.

"An unfair question, I agree," David said mockingly. "Like asking a girl if you may kiss her. Even liberated women find it difficult to shed the tradition that a woman should never advance, always retreat . . . however slowly."

The path was wide enough for several people to walk abreast, and other walkers were passing them as they stood there. Jane did not look at them, but she heard their voices. Some were chatting in French, some in Italian.

Disregarding the possibility that they might understand English, David added, "Perhaps I didn't kiss you last night to test the strength of your principles. True equality would mean that it wasn't always the man who had to take a chance of his advances being welcome. That's an aspect of equality which you have overlooked, I expect."

"I find it difficult to believe that you have to screw up your courage to . . . to kiss people." She glanced in the direction they were going. "The others are almost out of sight."

He laughed, and let her go. As they walked on, he said, "That isn't the point, my girl, and you know it. Do they let you get away with these red herrings at your university? The point we're discussing is not my courage, but yours. Let's suppose you had wanted to kiss me last night. You could have done so quite easily when I was replacing your hair fastening. But would you have dared to? And if not, why not? You ought to think these matters out if you're seriously opposed to the status quo of the man-woman relationship."

Jane saw Emma hopping and skipping along the path towards them. She turned to David, and said dulcetly, "Perhaps if you had wanted to kiss me, and had done so, I might have realised the folly of my advanced ideas, and the delights of being an old-fashioned, submissive girl."

His teeth showed white against his tan. "I expect there will be other opportunities to convert you."

"You two are dawdling today," said Emma, as she reached them. "We'd never have got to Mürren if you'd walked as slowly as this."

"We've been discussing the vagaries of mountain weather. It's particularly unpredictable around the Jungfrau," said her uncle, as he lengthened his stride. He cast a glinting glance at Jane. "However, I think I'm beginning to recognise some of the signs now."

Lake Oeschinen lapped a gently sloping shore on one side, and on the other reflected the formidable ramparts of the Rothorn, the Blümlisalphorn and the Oeschinenhorn, which rose almost sheer from the lake's far side.

A chalet-hotel, and a café, provided refreshments and souvenirs for visitors, and a line of rowing and motor boats was drawn up along the gravel beach near the main approach to the lake. But although this area was fairly crowded with sightseers, it was not difficult for Mrs. Wroxham's party to find a secluded spot for lunch.

As they were finishing their picnic, John said, "Don't put the banana skins in the rubbish bag, Mum. Give them to the cows. I was talking to the doctor in camp the other day, and she told me that Indian cows love banana skins. Perhaps Swiss cows do, too."

"I shouldn't think so," said Mary. "But we can try one on them." She tossed a banana skin towards a couple of cows who had ambled over to gaze at the picnic party.

Seconds after it had landed on the grass, the skin was being munched by the cow with the fastest reactions. The two animals which, up to then, had been standing at a polite distance, like curious but well brought up children, clearly regarded the banana skin as an invitation to join the party. In no time,

157

eight banana skins had been consumed with relish, and the Wroxhams were surrounded by half a dozen soft-eyed animals, all hopefully twitching their large, fringed ears, and mooing a summons to cows which, grazing further away, were missing these delicious yellow titbits.

When no more banana skins were forthcoming, the bolder beasts decided to try licking the people. Their large tickling tongues frightened Thomas and Francesca, but the older children found the experience hilarious and were disappointed when David and Jane succeeded in shooing the cows away. Their tongues had left sticky smears on everyone, and it was necessary to wash in the lake which, not surprisingly, was icy.

Late in the afternoon, returning to the *sesselbahn* by a different path, they saw the trail of disaster left by a winter avalanche. Huge, chalet-sized masses of rock had been wrenched away from the mountainside and, on their way down, had snapped the trunks of tall firs as if they were matchsticks.

"Goodness, I shouldn't care to live there," murmured Mary, indicating a chalet not far from the ravaged area.

Further along, half a dozen young pigs were rooting, knee-deep in buttercups. Ahead, Jane noticed, David was testing to see if Francesca liked butter. She wondered if he would contrive to share her chair-lift on the way down to Kandersteg. But he did not. This time she went alone.

In the late afternoon light of the late summer day, the mountains were unforgettably beautiful. A strange thought came into her mind. It was that if she were forced to crowd a lifetime into a single season of intense happiness, she would choose to spend a summer in the Berner Alps with David Carleton.

Jake Bedingfield was a short, thick-set man with prematurely grizzled hair. His voice was his only physical charm. Jane's thought, when they shook hands, was – What an unexpected husband for Fanny. But it did not take her long to realise that he had qualities of mind and character which made his lack of looks unimportant.

Throughout supper, he kept his family and guests on the brink of laughter. But one of his stories was a sad one. It was about a couple who, in the last century, had chosen Mürren for their honeymoon. They were both enthusiastic walkers, but on one excursion the bridegroom had left his young wife resting on a rock while he explored a higher path. In his absence, there was a sudden, violent storm of the kind which occur in mountain country. He returned to find her dead, struck by lightning.

"It's a true story," Fanny confirmed, when Mary looked doubtful. "There's a marker on the spot where it happened."

Although the Bedingfields urged them to stay for a second night, Mary thought it best to return to the camp.

There was a rainbow colouring the Staubbachfall when Jane went to the washroom next morning. As she brushed her teeth at the stainless steel trough, she looked through the window at the sun on the high snowfields, and the blue sky above the peaks. It was going to be another glorious day.

The children were keen to ride on another chair lift, and Mary decided to take them to Grindelwald, in the neighbouring valley, where according to Fanny there was a five-station hoist which carried passengers more than three thousand five hundred feet above the valley floor.

Grindelwald was the only mountain resort in that part of Switzerland which was accessible to cars, and it had several modern hotels, and a more sophisticated atmosphere than Lauterbrunnen. The valley in which it lay was like a shallow basin, unlike the typical glacier groove of the Lauterbrunnen gorge. As the Wroxhams strolled from the car park to the Firstbahn, Mary was inclined to think it a pity they had not made Grindelwald their base.

David bought return tickets to First, the highest point of the hoist, but they decided to break the journey at Bort, the third station. The valley surrounding Grindelwald was scattered with attractive old and new chalets, orchards and groves of maples. On the second stage of the journey, between the

159

Oberhaus station and Bort, they passed over fields where the country people were haymaking. The scent of the hay, the chirping of crickets, the glorious heatwave weather, and the grandeur of the views, on every side, of towering peaks and shimmering glaciers, combined into an experience which Jane felt sure she would remember for ever.

They had lunch by a rushing, bubbling stream. Afterwards the children picked flowers, dangled bare feet in the water, and explored the grassy slopes round about. The grown-ups lazed in the sun. David studied the white crest of the Fiescher-hörner through his binoculars. Mary dozed. Jane watched David, secure in the knowledge that, with sunglasses on, she would appear to be gazing at the scenery.

The view from the heights of First was even more spectacular, but the surrounding landscape was treeless and, to Jane's eyes, rather bleak compared with the Arcady of the alpine meadows.

When it was time to take the lift down to Grindelwald, David said, "You go with Francesca this time, will you, John."

Mary and Thomas, and the twins, had already begun their descent. As the attendant banged down the guard rails on the chair shared by John and his younger sister, Jane felt a pang of nervous excitement in the pit of her stomach.

"You don't mind coming with me, do you?" David asked blandly, but with a gleam in his eyes which reminded her of his teasing yesterday at Kandersteg.

As their chair swung out of the station, into the sunlight, it was not the sideways lurch which made her heart beat, but the prospect of being inescapably alone with him for the best part of half an hour.

However, after a few minutes, she found his company preferable to Francesca's, for with him beside her there was no chatter to distract her from the pleasure of gliding slowly, almost silently, down the cable.

It was near the station called Egg, when they had just skimmed above a little lake, that she broke the silence herself by exclaiming involuntarily, "Imagine living here … growing up here. No wonder Fanny and Jake are thinking of settling."

"You sound as if you'd fallen in love with Switzerland," he said, with an amused glance.

"I suppose I have. I should think most people do – except perhaps those who, like you, have travelled a great deal."

"I'm not immune. I had my first attack in the Ardennes whe I was sixteen," he answered. "When I was John's age, Europe was still in chaos, and as our parents had been separated throughout the war they preferred to stay put when it was over. The first time I crossed the Channel was with a party of senior schoolboys led by our French master. I learnt two important things on that trip. The first was that I seemed to have a diddicoy strain in me. Diddicoy is an old Norfolk name for a gypsy, or any wandering person," he added, in response to her puzzled look.

"And the second thing?"

"The second was a piece of Arab wisdom." David paused. " 'Life is shorter than Death'. And on that principle …" He finished the sentence by kissing her.

It was only a light, brief kiss, but its effect on Jane was as catastrophic as an avalanche. When it was over, when the pounding of her pulses was subsiding and she could think again, the world was a changed place, and all her plans were in ruins. Too late, much too late to retreat, she realised that she had fallen in love with him, not lightly, but with all her heart.

The next day, their last day in the valley, was disappointing. Low cloud discouraged them from planning an all-day expedition, and they spent the morning pottering about the camp in the hope that the weather might improve by lunch time.

After lunch, Mary said, "We can't allow our stay here to end on a low note. In spite of the clouds, it doesn't appear to be going to rain. How about holding a bangers-and-beans-feast this evening?"

Her suggestion was received with enthusiasm, and ten minutes later they were all in the van, heading for the Migros supermarket in Interlaken.

While they were in the town, Jane chanced to notice a German edition of Jane Austen's *Persuasion*. As she looked at the illustrated jacket, she recalled a sentence in the book which expressed, in a nutshell, the causes of her present predicament. *He had nothing to do, and she had hardly anybody to love.* She must have read that line a dozen times, never dreaming that one day she would find herself a victim of the same dangerous combination of masculine boredom and feminine loneliness.

Since yesterday afternoon she had managed to avoid being alone with David, but she was conscious of being watched by him, and she was sure that, sooner or later, he would contrive another *tête-à-tête*. Perhaps he derived a cat-and-mouse enjoyment from delaying the occasion. Oh, what a fool she had been to think she could play at love! Now she would have to pay for her recklessness with months of unhappiness.

It was as well that Mary bought plenty of frankfurters and bread rolls. When they returned to camp, four Scottish students were erecting a tent near the Wroxhams' pitch and, on learning that they were on their way home after working in a Munich bookbindery for most of the summer vacation, Mary invited them to the cook-out. With the American doctor and his wife, and the four Sussex caravanners who had replaced the departed Brundalls, there were eighteen people to be fed, no easy task on a twin-burner camp stove.

As she buttered the rolls while Mary cooked the sausages, Jane wished it were possible for her to slip inside the van and go to bed without anyone noticing her absence. She had slept hardly at all the night before, and now weariness was beginning to catch up with her.

"Can I give you a hand?" David asked her.

Jane, who had thought he was talking to the young Scots, gave a startled jump, followed by a gasp. In her nervousness at finding him behind her, not at a safe distance as she had supposed, she had gashed her left forefinger.

Although the cut was quite a deep one, it was pleasure not pain which she experienced while David administered first aid. But it was pleasure which she would have avoided if she could, for she knew instinctively that the more memories of him which she took back to England with her, the more protracted and painful would be her recovery. Throughout his ministrations she kept her eyes downcast, and as soon as he had finished she said a few clipped words of thanks, and moved away. She did not speak to him again, or he to her, that evening.

Next day they broke camp, and began the long journey home. Mary had decided that Heidelberg would be an interesting and romantic place to stay on the way back, but it was a long day's drive from the Valley of Waterfalls, and by the time they arrived everyone was tired. The camp where they spent that night was several kilometres outside the town, on the bank of the river Neckar. At first they were so glad to have reached their destination that the disadvantages of the place did not make much impact.

"What a pity we can't all fit inside the van. It's rather a chore having to put a tent up at the end of a long day like this one," said Mary to Jane, as they set out the cooking equipment while David and the three eldest children performed the now familiar routine of fitting the metal tubes of the frame together.

It was only when the tent had been erected, and it was too late to have second thoughts, that they began to be fully aware that the peaceful impression given by the thickly wooded hills beside the river was decidedly illusory. Not only did the river have a considerable amount of barge traffic but, on the far bank, there was a busy railway line and, beyond that, a four-lane highway.

It was not raining when they woke the following morning, but obviously it had rained for some hours in the night. The grass was sodden, and there were pools of water on the path to the camp office and washrooms.

"We can't leave until the tent has had time to dry," said David, when Mary proposed an early departure.

"Supposing the sun never gets out today? I couldn't stand another night like last night. The traffic seems never to stop here."

By ten o'clock, she had prevailed on her brother to move. But as David had feared, it was impossible to dismantle and fold a large expanse of canvas in such conditions without both the tent and its handlers becoming much muddied. To make matters worse, it began to drizzle.

"Oh, dear, now he's annoyed," murmured Mary, watching David stride away to the washroom when, at last, the tent had been packed.

Possibly on a bright morning, after an undisturbed night, they might have liked Heidelberg. But after exploring the town for an hour, they were not sorry to continue their journey north.

By the time they stopped for a picnic lunch in the parking lines of a *rasthof*, the sun was shining and everyone felt more cheerful. Only David remained taciturn.

"I think tonight we should try to find a rural camping," remarked Mary, consulting her site guide. "Somewhere well away from the *autobahn* or any large town."

"How many nights are there left, Mummy?" Emma asked her.

"Only two camping nights, darling. On Monday we shall reach the Hague, and our nice boarding house where we always stay. And on Tuesday we shall be on board the *Duke of Holland*. Looking back on the whole trip, I don't think we can complain, do you? Yesterday was rather disagreeable, but most of the holiday has been nice, and several days have been glorious. The day we took the chair-lift up the mountain above Grindelwald, for instance. That was unforgettable, wasn't it?"

The children, their mouths full of bread and cheese, nodded agreement.

"Do you second that, Jane?" enquired David. "Was it unforgettable for you?"

Because of his withdrawn mood, she had been off guard. To look up and find him watching her with quizzical eyes was like walking into an ambush. With an effort, she answered coolly, "I preferred the day at Oeschinen."

At mid-afternoon, they left the ceaseless flow of cars along the *autobahn* and followed a minor road through pleasant, undulating farmlands until the drone of heavy traffic was lost in the distance, and it was hard to believe that not very far to the north were the coalfields and chimneys of the industrial Ruhr region.

The camp for which they were heading was called Lochmühle, which Mary took to be the name of a lake. But David said that in German *loch* meant a hole, and *mühle* was a mill.

They found the camp at the end of a long, private lane which crossed a stream where a man was fishing from the bridge, passed between a coppice and a field of Indian corn, and finally came to an end in the forecourt of a building part farmhouse and part *gasthof*.

"Ah, now *this* is more like it!" said Mary in a satisfied tone, as they climbed out and stretched their legs, and found that here there were no diesel fumes, only pleasant farmyard odours, and no deafening barge hooters or train whistles, only the gurgle of the mill-race.

"What's more, I shan't need to cook tonight," she added, after studying a menu posted outside the entrance to the establishment.

Within an hour of their arrival the tent was pitched in the meadow used by transient campers, and the canvas was sufficiently dry for David to start brushing off the mud. Soon there was little trace of the day's disorderly beginning.

They dined on a dish called *Jägerschnitzel* which consisted of a large, tender cutlet with a lavish accompaniment of mushrooms, tomatoes, green peas and golden-brown chips.

As they strolled back to the meadow, past a cluster of

permanently-parked caravans, some of them sprouting TV aerials, the night air had an autumnal nip. No one else had arrived to share the meadow.

"Perhaps not many foreign campers discover this place. It is rather tucked away," said Mary. "David, would it be a good idea to spend tomorrow night here as well, and to finish the journey in one last, long run on Monday? If we move tomorrow, we may not be lucky a second time."

"Suits me," he answered laconically.

On Sunday they were woken by the soft lowing of the cattle in the barns behind the farmhouse. It was a hot, cloudless morning and, after breakfast, when the dew had dried and David had given it another brushing, the tent looked as clean as it had at the beginning of the holiday.

His next task was to wash the van, helped by the children until some unexpected entertainment was provided by trainees for the local Fire Brigade. They arrived at mid-morning to practise unrolling and directing hoses on the far side of the meadow. Even Mary and Jane deserted their chores for a while to watch the two groups of young men dashing about while an experienced fireman called out instructions and timed their exertions with a stop-watch.

But although, apart from this distraction, the adult members of the English party were busy all morning, their activities were leisurely compared with the frenzy of grass-cutting, fence-painting, car-washing, car-tinkering and other odd-jobbery being done by the occupants of the caravans.

"Goodness! They don't have much of a rest, do they?" murmured Mary, as she and Jane strolled to the farm outbuilding which had been converted into a shop selling sweets, ice creams and soft drinks.

"If they come from big cities like Cologne and Frankfurt, merely being in the open air in these quiet surroundings must refresh them," said David, causing his sister to jump because she had not realised he was behind them.

Jane had not realised it either. She gave no outward sign of

166

being startled, but her heart lurched in the way it always did now when he came upon her unexpectedly.

"Yes, it's a peaceful spot," agreed Mary, pausing to shade her eyes with her hand and survey the wooded slope which sheltered the crescent-curve of the trout stream. "How lucky we were to find it! It would have been a shame to finish the holiday in a camp as dreary as the one near Heidelberg."

The reminder that in a little more than forty-eight hours they would be at sea filled Jane with mingled dismay and relief. David had not mentioned his plans for the rest of his leave, but she felt sure that he did not intend to linger under his brother-in-law's roof. Probably he would spend Wednesday night in Norfolk, and on Thursday morning he would say good-bye, and that would be the last she would ever see of him. Even if he returned to the Wroxhams' home at the end of his furlough, she would no longer be there.

"I'd better look at your cut," he said to her.

"It's almost healed."

"Have you taken off the dressing, and looked?"

"No, but I can feel that it has."

"I'll look at it . . . if you don't mind."

She did mind. To submit, with outward unconcern, to the touch of his strong brown fingers called for all her self-control. She managed not to show any reaction, but later in the day her control was put to a stiffer test, which it failed.

After lunch, the grown-ups were lazing in the sun, and the children were petting an enchanting St. Bernard puppy which belonged to the farm, when Mary remembered that they still had two or three unused films in the camera.

"David, could you ask the man in the nearest caravan if he would take a photo of all seven of us?" she asked.

"I'll take a snap of the rest of you."

"No, no, I want you to be included. Do you realise we haven't a single photograph of you?"

After some argument, he was persuaded to do as she wished, and their neighbour not only agreed to the request, but was clearly delighted to demonstrate his photographic expertise.

Dissatisfied with their first grouping, he directed various rearrangements.

"The sun will have set if he doesn't buck up," David said, in an undertone to Jane.

He was standing between her and his sister, behind John and the twins, with Francesca and Thomas at the front.

Satisfied at last with their placing, the German had only one more instruction to give them. Flapping both hands, he motioned them to move nearer together.

"With pleasure." David put his arm round Jane and drew her close to his side.

It was at once the most blissful and the most unbearable sensation, and her reactions were equally mixed. In swift succession she yielded, then jerked away, then yielded again, but stiffly, her whole body rigid. The time required for two snapshots seemed like five minutes.

Afterwards it was necessary for David to thank the German, and chat to him. Perhaps he hadn't noticed her rigidity, Jane thought hopefully. But she felt in her bones that he had noticed, and that he was not the sort of man who would accept being treated as if he didn't wash or had bad teeth. How stupid of her to recoil like that! Probably his other arm had been round his sister's waist, and if Jane hadn't tensed the gesture would have had no significance.

By half past five most of the caravanners were preparing to leave. Camp chairs were folded away, curtains were drawn, gaily coloured track suits taken off and sober lounge suits put on. Couple by couple, family by family, they locked their immaculate caravans, closed the gates in the fences surrounding their garden plots, and set forth in their cars for the workaday world of the city.

The Wroxhams had supper in the *gasthof* restaurant, and only one other table was occupied. Like the caravanners, most of the hotel guests seemed to have been weekend visitors.

After supper, David leaned on the bar counter and talked

to the proprietor and another local man. Jane and Mary played dominoes with the children. Once Jane looked up and saw David staring at her, his eyes narrowed, his expression curiously ominous.

The camp washrooms were close to the flight of steps leading down from the restaurant to the forecourt. When the children had been put to bed, the two women returned to wash themselves. David was still at the bar.

There was only one shower compartment, and Mary took the first turn while Jane washed some smalls. By the time Jane had finished her shower, Mary had gone back to the van.

When Jane emerged from the washroom, she was surprised and perturbed to see David standing on the bridge across the mill-stream. Instantly she felt certain that he was waiting for her. The only way to avoid him was to circle round behind the farmhouse. But without a torch it would not be easy to find the way and, if that engaging young St. Bernard had his kennel somewhere at the back of the buildings, and she blundered past it, he might start to bark and alert everyone for miles around.

Anyway, perhaps David wasn't waiting for her. She had no reason to think that he was, only her instinct, and the memory of that searching stare he had fixed on her earlier.

Her instinct had not misled her. As she made to walk past him, meaning to say a casual good night, he barred her path.

"I want to talk to you."

"Now?"

"It's not late."

"No, but Mary may be tired, and wanting to put out the light."

"If she's as tired as that, the light won't keep her awake. She's been known to sleep through Peter's night calls. It's too cool to stand about. We'll walk as far as the other bridge. There and back won't take five minutes."

"But I don't –" Her objection petered out as he gripped her firmly behind the elbow, and propelled her across the lighted forecourt to the more shadowy lane bordered on one side by trees, on the other by the field of tall maize. She knew it was useless to protest. If he wanted to talk to her, he would. But what about?

He did not keep her in suspense. "We seem to have entered a second ice age," he said, in his most sardonic tone. "Don't pretend not to know what I mean. Ever since we came down the mountain together at Grindelwald, you've been freezing again. At the risk of being frostbitten, I want to know why?"

As he said, it was pointless to prevaricate. "Because I don't want to be involved in a holiday flirtation, that's why!"

"You seemed to have no such scruples the night we dined at Brienz."

"Well, I have now," she said childishly, trying to pull free.

He halted and swung her to face him, grasping her other arm. "And I object to being treated like a vile seducer for a kiss that was no more than friendly! It's time you learnt to take life – and yourself! – a great deal less seriously, my girl."

"Will you please let me go," Jane said, wincing. His fingers were painfully strong.

He did, but only for a moment. An instant later, he had one arm round her waist and his other hand under her chin, forcing her to look up at him. "Perhaps you find this more comfortable?" – pulling her closer.

She swallowed, suddenly frightened not only of him in this mood, but of the wayward emotions he aroused in her. She said angrily, "No, I do not!" in a desperate attempt to revive her weakening resistance.

"I won't keep you long," he said smoothly. "But if you're determined to shun me, I may as well justify my odium." Then, slowly and thoroughly, he kissed her.

When he lifted his head, Jane was shaking. The moonlight fell on her face, but his was in shadow, unreadable. Knowing what her face must reveal, she tore herself free of his slackened grasp, and ran back the way they had come.

Some yards from the van, she halted, realising that she

must have time to compose herself before Mary saw her. A nervous glance over her shoulder showed no sign of David following her. When her self-control seemed equal to facing his sister, she entered the van. To her surprise and relief, Mary was already asleep. Jane crept quietly into her sleeping bag and turned off the light. But it was hours before she slept.

It was a five-hour drive from Lochmühle to The Hague the next day, but there was a cordial welcome awaiting them from the Dutch couple who ran the comfortable boarding house on the Zwijgerlaan where the Wroxhams had stayed on several previous occasions.

"How these children have grown since last time you were here," exclaimed Mevrouw Verhoeven, in her excellent English, as she showed them upstairs to their bedrooms.

The prospect of supper at a *snackroom* soon revived the children's energy, and for once they needed little urging to wash and change.

"What a civilized nation the Dutch are," said Mary, when they were walking to the *snackroom*. "Even here in the suburbs there's a bookshop and florist on nearly every street. Did you ever see such clean windows and spotless curtains? I like the way, after dark, they leave their curtains open. It's so much more cheerful than our way. It gives me a Christmassy feeling."

It was as well that Mrs. Wroxham was in animated spirits, because neither David nor Jane contributed much to the evening's gaiety. The children chattered away as usual, and David responded to remarks specifically addressed to him. But Jane was so sunk in misery that making conversation was quite beyond her. The best she could do was to say Yes and No, and to pretend to enjoy her *loempia*, a crisp batter parcel of shredded chicken and bean shoots accompanied by chips served with sea salt and fresh mayonnaise. In fact she was not at all hungry.

As they were leaving the *snackroom*, David said, "If you don't mind, Mary, I think I'll take off for a couple of hours."

"Did you ask Mevrouw Verhoeven for a key? I think they they lock up at midnight."

"I'll be back before then. Good night, children." He walked away along the wide, square-tiled pavement.

"Where is he going? Can't we go, too?" asked Emma.

"I expect he feels like a quiet drink away from all you chatterboxes," answered her mother.

But as the rest of them turned in the opposite direction, Jane saw Mrs. Wroxham glance over her shoulder at her brother's tall figure with a wrinkle between her eyebrows.

Walking back to the boarding house, Mary said, "This time tomorrow night we shall be at sea. Much as I've enjoyed the trip, I shan't be sorry to be home again. Three weeks is too long to be separated from Peter. How about you, Jane? Are you glad or sorry that the holiday is almost over?"

Jane found it difficult to know how to answer. Her hesitation caused Mary to continue, "I suppose you have mixed feelings, too? Like me, you've enjoyed it; but while I'm looking forward to saying hello to my husband, you're looking forward to saying good-bye to my brother. Am I right?"

Jane gave her a startled glance. "What makes you think that?"

"You told me before we came abroad that you didn't like him. You expressed it more tactfully, but I fancy that was what you really meant, wasn't it?"

The children, who had stopped to gaze in the window of a toyshop, came scampering to join the two women. Their presence saved Jane from answering the awkward question, and perhaps others even more awkward.

She and Mary and the two little girls were sharing a bedroom at the back of the boarding house. Long after the other three were asleep, Jane lay awake in the dark, listening to their peaceful breathing, and wondering where David had gone.

About half past eleven she heard a stair creak, and the almost inaudible click of a door being opened further along the landing. The intimacy of camp life made it easy for her to

172

visualise David's preparations for bed in the adjoining room. Many times, passing the men's washrooms, she had glimpsed him shaving, or seen his strong, sun-tanned back bent over a handbasin. But although she could imagine him folding his clothes, washing, and cleaning his teeth, she had no means of knowing if, when the clock in the hall chimed midnight, he was still awake. Although the memory of being in his arms kept her awake until the small hours, it didn't seem likely that David was losing any sleep over the episode at Lochmühle.

At breakfast, they discussed how to spend the morning. Emma wanted to visit the Gemeente Museum to see a doll's house which Willem Hoogveld had described to her the day they went over the Sustenpass.

At her mention of Willem, David said, "Ah, yes – Jane's swain. I'd forgotten about him."

So had Jane. Her short acquaintance with the young Dutchman seemed an aeon ago.

As if he read her mind, David asked, "Had you forgotten him, too, Jane? Has that romantic evening at Lucerne faded from your mind so soon? Surely not?"

His tone had such a cutting edge that even the children noticed it, and stared at his sardonic face and then, in puzzlement, at Jane's flushed one.

"What about you, John? Have you any suggestions?" asked Mary, apparently deaf to her brother's barbed remark.

A boy at his school, who had been to Holland last year, had told John about a museum specialising in instruments of torture, and this, he thought, would be much more interesting than dolls' houses. The twins, when they were consulted, wanted to spend the morning on the beach at Scheveningen, the holiday resort adjacent to the Hague. In the end, Mary decided to follow Mevrouw Verhoeven's suggestion and take a tram to the Hague's large, open-air market.

"Will you come with us, David?" she enquired. "Or doesn't the market appeal to you?"

"I'll come," he replied.

On the opposite side of the table, Jane sprinkled a spoonful of chocolate *hagel* on Thomas's bread and butter, and felt an irrational sense of reprieve. Common sense might tell her that the sooner she saw the last of David the better it would be for her, but it could not stop her from hoping that somehow something might yet happen which, when finally they shook hands, would make him look at her less coldly than he had a few moments ago. She felt she could not bear it if the last time he ever looked at her, his eyes held that glacial mockery. It no longer mattered to her that, morally, she was the one who was justified in looking icy. As the last hours of the holiday fled away, she found it impossible to sustain any sense of outrage at being kissed against her will.

As soon as they stepped off the tram at the entrance to the market, they noticed a strong scent of citrus fruits. On every stall selling fruit, there were oranges, lemons and grapefruit cut open to show the luscious juiciness of the flesh, and the air was full of their zest. The children, who had thought the market would be dull, discovered that many of the wares were things they had never seen before, although their uncle recognised them. There were mangoes and durians from the East, buckets of tender green bean shoots, and several varieties of banana. Beyond the alleys of produce stalls were stalls spread with bronze mounds of smoked fish. Presently they stopped at a mobile coffee stall where David bought everyone a sizzling-hot apple fritter.

"Take care you don't burn your fingers," he warned, handing one to his sister and another to Jane.

I already have, she thought wanly.

At the back of the market they found a flea market selling second-hand books and old clothes, and a fascinating muddle of bric-à-brac gleaned from the city's attics. Here everyone was happy to dawdle, even Thomas who, while the others were treasure-hunting, was happily engaged in attempting to stroke the market pigeons.

174

From the market, they walked to the city centre to look at the shops. But an hour of this was more than enough for the children and, while they were lunching in a restaurant, David offered to take them to the zoo at Wassenaar so that Mary and Jane could continue to window-shop at leisure.

"That's a splendid idea. We'll meet you at the boarding house at half past four," agreed Mary.

Shortly after the party had split up, she decided that, if Jane had no objection to being on her own for an hour or two, she would have her hair done. "Why don't you join me?" she suggested.

"No, I don't think I will, if you don't mind. Perhaps I'll go to see the paintings in the Maurithuis."

Luckily, the first hairdressing salon they tried was able to fit Mary in.

"Shall I meet you here, or at the boarding house?" asked Jane, before they parted.

"At the boarding house would be best. I'm not sure what time I'll be finished here. They may be quick, or very slow. You aren't likely to get lost, are you?"

"No, I know where to catch the tram. I shan't lose my way," Jane assured her.

In the end, feeling no more inclined to gaze at Old Masters than to fidget under a hair-dryer, she passed the next couple of hours wandering aimlessly about the city, wondering how long it would take her to overcome her present wretchedness.

It seemed to her that everywhere she looked there were men and girls sitting on benches or strolling, hands clasped, shoulders close, gazing into each other's eyes.

For a time she sat in a pavement café, sipping black coffee, until glancing at her watch she discovered that it was later than she had realised, and time to return to the tram stop in Grote Markt Straat.

Five minutes later, as, thinking of David, she turned to cross a busy street, the habit of years reasserted itself. She looked to the right, not the left. Simultaneously, Jane heard a scream of warning, and was flung off her feet by a violent impact. Then something else struck her head, and the world became a whirlpool of crimson light which sucked her down into nothingness.

CHAPTER VII

AFTERWARDS, when she was asked what she remembered of the twenty-four hours following the accident, Jane described the experience as something like being in a dark room, facing a television which most of the time was switched off, but which occasionally turned itself on to show a brief and rather confusing snatch of programme.

The first time this happened the screen was badly out of focus, and the face which she saw was so blurred that it was only by the voice that she knew it was a woman who was speaking to her.

The voice was quiet and kind. It said, "You have had an accident, and now you are in hospital. Don't worry. We will take care of you. You will feel better soon . . . don't worry . . ."

Then both face and voice faded away, and there was darkness and silence for a time.

The next time, the voice repeated the reassurances, and the face was a little less blurred. Presently there were two faces. The second person was a man who also spoke kindly to her. By now, in spite of a headache, Jane's mind was sufficiently clear for her to recognise the woman as a nurse, and the man as a doctor. But there was something about them which puzzled her. It was difficult to think while her head was throbbing, but suddenly she knew what was "wrong" about them. They were speaking to her in English, but they were not English.

"Where am I?" she asked. "*Where am I?*"

They told her she was in hospital in The Hague in Holland. They told her that her name was Jane Winfarthing, and she had been knocked down by a car and had hit her head, but was otherwise not seriously injured. They told her to rest, and not to worry if she could not remember the accident or what had preceded it. This was not unusual. Her memory would clear quite soon, they promised.

Nevertheless it was strange, and rather frightening, not to be able to remember how she had come to be knocked down, or even what she had been doing in The Hague. But she accepted what they told her and did not worry until, gradually, out of the thick fog obscuring the past, there came a feeling that at the time of the accident she had been on her way to . . . where?

As the sense of urgency increased, she did begin to worry. The more she thought about it, the more she was convinced that she had been on an errand of great importance, that some kind of time limit or deadline was involved, and that even now it might not be too late to get there . . . if only she could remember where "there" was, and why it was so important.

"Nurse! Nurse, I must get up. Where are my clothes?" As she struggled up on to her elbows, the pain in her head was like a lance piercing her skull.

She gasped, and fine beads of sweat broke out on her forehead. When the nurse made her lie down again, she did not resist, but tears of frustration and confusion welled up in her eyes.

"I'll be too late. They'll have gone . . . they'll have gone without me."

"Who will have gone, Miss Winfarthing?" Now it was the doctor who was leaning towards her.

But whatever she had glimpsed through the mists in her mind was no longer there. "I don't know. I can't remember," she said helplessly.

"Never mind. You will remember in time," he assured her.

She heard him giving instructions to the nurse, and then his voice died away and it was dark again.

The next time she opened her eyes, her headache seemed to have spread throughout her body. After a few minutes she came to the conclusion that it was better to feel sore everywhere than to have that dreadful, drill-like agony in her head.

Presently, when the nurse came to look at her, she asked, "Was I alone when the car hit me? Wasn't there anyone with me?"

"There was no person with you, Jane. We think you were buying souvenirs to take home from your holiday here. Perhaps you had arranged to meet your family, or your friends, when your shopping was finished. Perhaps for tea, perhaps not until the evening. If that is so, it will not be long before they find you. When someone is missing, it is always at the hospital that the search begins. Very soon you will see faces you know. Don't worry. Don't cry."

Jane sniffed, and managed a wan smile. But after the nurse had gone, she could not help crying. She closed her eyes but the tears squeezed under her eyelids and trailed down her cheeks. Even if she could not remember any details yet, she knew in her bones that she was alone now, that the others had gone on without her, and that, because of the accident, there was someone she might never see again. . . someone important . . . someone who . . .

After a long time in darkness, she roused. Presently, a hand lifted her left hand from where it lay on the sheet, not in order to feel her pulse, but to sandwich her cold, lax fingers between two warm palms

A voice said tentatively, "Jane?"

She opened her eyes and saw, through a shimmer of tears, a tall, tanned man with dark hair. It was a moment of joyous recognition in which she knew with perfect certainty that here was the one person who, in all the world, mattered most to her.

And with that rock-like conviction to hold to, it seemed unimportant that she could not recall his name, or the nature of their relationship.

With a sigh of contentment, she fell asleep.

When she woke, her mind was clear, her memory restored.

"Ah, I see you feel better, Miss Winfarthing," said a nurse, coming into the small, sunny private room where her patient was trying to sit up.

"Yes, much better, thank you," said Jane, as the nurse came to aid her. "But I don't know how long I've been here. Was I brought in yesterday?"

"No, for two nights you have been here. On Tuesday was the accident, and now it is Thursday morning. But for the first twenty-four hours you were not often conscious, and after that you were sleeping most of the time."

"I thought someone was here ... an Englishmen called David Carleton. Or did I only imagine that?" Jane asked urgently.

The Dutch girl smiled. "No, Mr. Carleton was here, and soon you will see him again. But after being here at the hospital for many hours while you were unconscious, he must be very tired. I think this morning he too will sleep a long time. He is staying at a hotel not far away."

Later, when a doctor came to see her, Jane learned that David had arrived at the hospital within two hours of her own admission. He had told the doctor that his sister and her children had returned to England as planned, but that he intended to stay at The Hague until Jane was fit to go home.

"How soon will that be, doctor?" Jane asked anxiously.

"That I cannot yet say, Miss Winfarthing," he said cautiously. "When there has been severe concussion, a period of rest is advisable. Also you have many bruises. Mr. Carleton tells me there is no urgent reason for either of you to return to England. We must see how you progress."

It was mid-morning when the nurse put her head round the door to tell Jane that Mr. Carleton was on his way up in the lift. A few moments later there was a knock, and David himself walked in.

"Hello, Jane. I hear you're feeling more yourself. I've brought one or two things you may need," he remarked, as he came to the bedside. He placed several parcels on the locker, pulled up a chair, and sat down and surveyed her more closely.

"Well, you certainly look very different from when I first saw you in here. You had me quite worried for a while," he said, in a pleasant tone.

"I know. I feel terrible about it. Poor Mary! She must have been frantic when I didn't turn up at the rendezvous. What a nuisance I've been to you all. Especially to you . . . ruining the last part of your leave."

"Stop fussing, and open the parcels and see if the nighties are your size," David said calmly. "For the second time on this trip, you're without a rag to your back, my child. So am I, for that matter. I managed to convince Mary that her best course was to take the children home, and leave me to look after you. But we were so much concerned with finding you that we forgot that my kit and yours was stowed in the van."

Jane noticed that he was wearing a shirt and trousers which she had never seen before. "Oh, dear, and so you've had to buy new clothes. I've cost you money as well as wrecking your plans," she exclaimed, in dismay.

"Nonsense. I had no plans to be wrecked. There's no need for you to worry about the expense of your treatment here. Mary isn't fool enough to go on holiday without adequate medical insurance for everyone in the party." As he talked, he unwrapped one of the parcels and tossed its contents on to her lap.

With mingled pleasure and concern – for they were not cheap, chain-store garments – she unfolded two short white nighties of fine cotton voile, and a blue and white short-length, frilled robe. Another parcel contained a pair of blue terry bath mules and a shower cap, and in the third package were various toilet articles, including a bottle of French toilet water, a folding mirror, tissues, and a bristle hairbrush.

"You've thought of everything," she said gratefully, rather overcome by the extravagance of his provision for her needs. "I don't know how to thank you."

"By not worrying about anything," David replied firmly. "I daresay your head still aches a good deal, but if you should

181

want something to read, I thought this might do for the time being." He tapped a paper bag which obviously contained a book. But before Jane could discover what he had chosen for her, he went on, "I was told not to stay for more than ten minutes, but I'll look in again later on. Meanwhile I'll telephone Mary, and tell her she can stop worrying, too. See you later, Jane." And giving her hand an encouraging pat, he rose to his feet and departed.

When he had gone, Jane fingered the pretty material of the blue and white peignoir, and fought against a strong urge to burst into tears. For although his manner could not have been kinder, it was deflatingly clear that her recollection of his previous visit to her bedside was far from accurate.

When she had opened her eyes and recognised him, in spite of being unable to remember his name, there had seemed to be a look in his eyes which she had hoped to see again this morning. But it was evident now that the look she remembered was no more than a piece of wishful thinking which, in her concussed state, had seemed real.

The nurse came, admired the new nightdresses, and helped Jane to put one on in place of the plain, tape-tied gown supplied by the hospital. It was surprising how exhausted Jane felt after this slight exertion. She was glad to lie down and doze for an hour.

It was not until after a light lunch that she remembered the book David had brought her. It was not a paperback as she had anticipated, but a hardcover copy of *Mansfield Park* by Jane Austen. The thoughtfulness which had made him take the trouble, in a foreign city, to search for an English edition of a novel which he knew to be one of her favourites gave her a warm sense of pleasure, until she reflected that perhaps he was being particularly nice to her now to atone for his rather brutal treatment at Lochmühle.

An interval of four days, and a stunning crack on the head, had not, she discovered, made the memory of Sunday night any less disturbing. She had only to close her eyes to recall, with most potent clarity, the hardness of his arm imprisoning her, the roughness of his cheek against hers when she tried to avert her face, and the unexpected softness of his lips once she had ceased to resist him.

About five o'clock in the afternoon when, for the first time, she was finding it difficult to become absorbed in the problems of the inhabitants of Mansfield Park, the nurse announced briefly, "A visitor for you, Miss Winfarthing."

But it was not David who presently appeared, bearing a large bouquet of flowers.

"Willem!" Jane cried, in astonishment. "What are you doing here?"

"I would have come sooner, but the hospital would not permit. Poor Jane. It is very bad luck that your holiday ends in this manner," Willem commiserated.

"But how did you know I was in here? Has David been in touch with you?"

"No, I have not heard from Mr. Carleton. I read of your accident in *Haagsche Courant*. It is news when an English girl is hurt a short time before she must catch the boat."

"I suppose so. Anyway, it's very kind of you to come to see me. The flowers are lovely. Thank you, Willem."

She was sniffing their scent when another knock heralded David's entrance.

"Good evening, Mr. Carleton." Willem offered his hand to the taller man. "I have been telling Jane that her name has been in the newspapers."

"Good evening." If David was surprised to find the young Dutchman with her, he did not show it, or any other reaction. After shaking hands, he turned towards the bed. "How now, Jane?"

"Apart from one or two bruises, I'm back to normal. I'll get up tomorrow."

"Hm . . . we'll see what the doctors have to say about that. You don't look too sprightly to me."

"My mother sends a message that, when you are permitted
183

to leave the hospital, she would be delighted to welcome you to our house for as long as you wish," Willem told Jane. "Perhaps it is not convenient for you to stay in Holland until Jane is ready to travel, Mr. Carleton. In that case we should be very happy to take care of her.''

"It's extremely kind of your mother, Willem," Jane began. "But –"

"But no inconvenience arises," David cut in briskly. "By the way, Mary has been in touch with your people, Jane. She got their address from the University, and talked to your mother on the telephone."

"Oh . . . did she? That was good of her."

Feeling very ungrateful in the face of his sympathetic concern, Jane wished Willem would go away. In spite of her vaunted normality, she was not feeling equal to visitors, other than David; and now that he had arrived, Willem's presence was a strain which made her feel limp.

Perhaps this showed in her face. Presently David said, "I think Jane is tired now, Hoogveld. Shall we leave her in peace? Whatever she may say, she is not well yet." Barely allowing Willem time to say good-bye, he steered the young man out of the room.

After supper, the doctor came to see her. "I hear you have eaten very little, Miss Winfarthing. Is that because you have no appetite? Or because the food doees not please you?"

"The supper was excellent. I'm just not hungry."

The doctor felt her pulse, examined her eyelids and her tongue, and then perched on the bedside and chatted. "Ah, Jane Austen: I also am an admirer of this writer," he said, picking up her book. "And Henry James I enjoy. You are familiar with his novels?"

For ten minutes he discussed his favourite books until, glancing at his watch, he stood up, saying, "I expected to find your fiancé with you. But perhaps he goes to bed early tonight."

"My fiancé? You mean David Carleton, Doctor?"

"Yes, Mr. Carleton."

"What made you think we were engaged?"

"It is what he has told me. It is not so?"

Jane shook her head.

The doctor gave a slightly puzzled shrug. "Perhaps Mr. Carleton felt it would make your position more *convenable*, as the French say. But it is unusual for you younger people to worry about the conventions of my generation. My children inform me that people of my age have very unpleasant minds, and see evil where none exists. Perhaps they are right. I must leave you. Good night, Miss Winfarthing."

Jane was seated in a chair by the window when David came to see her the following morning. He brought magazines, peaches, and a bottle of lime juice.

"You're losing weight," he observed, when she had thanked him. "Did you have some breakfast this morning?"

"Yes, a boiled egg and some toast." She had been expecting him for an hour, and now that he had arrived, her curiosity could be restrained no longer.

"David, the staff here seem to be under the impression that we are engaged. When I tried to explain, the doctor said you had *told* him I was your fiancée."

He returned her gaze, but he did not say anything, and the expression on his face was the one she could never fathom.

"Was that necessary?" she went on hurriedly. "Would they have thought it peculiar for you to stay in Holland with me . . . merely as a friend?"

"Probably not. I don't know. Do you find the part of my future wife a particularly objectionable one to play?"

"No, not objectionable. But to be in a false position is always a little uncomfortable."

"It isn't a false position as far as I'm concerned."

"W-what do you mean?"

"I wish very much that we *were* going to be married," he said. "But I don't think you feel the same way." He leaned

185

forward in his chair and took her hands. "Sometimes I think you love me, and sometimes I think you loathe me. Perhaps you aren't certain yourself?"

"Yes, I am," said Jane unsteadily.

And then, for the first time, his face revealed all that he was feeling. She realised, with amazement and consternation, that he was in a state of anxiety every bit as tense as the anguished uncertainty from which she was now, suddenly, free.

"Oh, David . . . I love you, of course! How could I not?"

"Very easily, I should have thought." He raised her hands and kissed first one and then the other. "But if you are certain of your feelings, why have you been at such pains to conceal them from me?"

"Because it seemed impossible that you could love me, and I couldn't bear to be just another scalp on your belt."

"What has given you this curious conviction that I'm a tremendous womaniser? It's completely unfounded," he told her. "No normal man reaches my age without being involved once or twice. But a succession of casual affairs doesn't appeal to anyone of moderate intelligence, you know. One looks for a permanent relationship. But sometimes it takes a long time to find the right girl."

"Am I really the right girl for you? I can't believe it," she murmured, in a daze of happiness.

It was at this point that the doctor entered the room. Seeing their clasped hands, and the expression on his patient's face, he said, with a twinkle, "I have the impression that it was not I but you who was mistaken last night, Miss Winfarthing. I do not need to enquire how you are feeling this morning."

"Doctor, is Jane fit to undertake a short journey?" David asked him. "Instead of returning to England by sea, I intend to go by air. My sister's home is in Norfolk, less than half an hour's drive from Norwich Airport. With a taxi from here to Amsterdam, the whole journey should not take more than a couple of hours. My brother-in-law is a doctor, so Jane would still be under medical supervision."

186

"In that case, I see no objection," the doctor replied. "I would advise Miss Winfarthing to continue to rest for several days, but I do not think there will be any more effects from her accident. If there are, your brother-in-law will quickly recognise the signs, and know how to treat them. Yes, you have my consent to your plan, Mr. Carleton. When do you propose to leave Holland? Tomorrow?"

"Today, if possible. I'll go and make enquiries. I shan't be long, darling," said David, squeezing Jane's hand.

Within an hour he had made all the necessary arrangements and, at noon, hoping that she was not suffering from a delightful hallucination, Jane found herself strolling to his hotel for lunch.

"I hope Mary will approve," she said, a trifle anxiously. "It's sure to be a great shock to her. I hope it won't be an unpleasant one."

"She didn't sound surprised when I told her about us," said David. He had telephoned his sister to ask if she could meet their flight, or if he should bring Jane home by taxi.

"Oh, you've already broken it to her? What did she say?"

"Nothing. She relayed the news to someone else – Peter, I expect – and then the operator asked if we wanted extra time, and Mary said 'See you this evening', and rang off. But of course she'll be pleased, my lovely. She's been wanting me to marry for years."

Yes, but not necessarily someone like me, thought Jane.

They were met at Norwich Airport by Doctor and Mrs. Wroxham, and all five children.

"Jane, my dear – I couldn't be more delighted," said Mary, embracing her affectionately. "In fact the only thing which made the holiday bearable for me without Peter was watching you two fall in love."

"You knew?" Jane exclaimed.

"Let's say I had strong suspicions, in spite of your doing your utmost to hide the fact from each other. When David began to paw the ground every time that poor young Dutchman appeared, and you drew even further inside your shell, it didn't call for great shrewdness to recognise the state of the parties."

Jane's smile changed to a look of dismay. "I'd forgotten about Willem. Oh, dear! How rude to come away without leaving a letter, or telephoning his office. He visited me in hospital, and brought a huge bunch of flowers," she explained to Mary.

"I didn't forget him. I left an explanatory note at the porter's lodge for him," David told her.

"Talking of the hospital, we mustn't forget that Jane is still not completely fit," intervened Doctor Wroxham. "The sooner we get you home the better, my dear."

On the drive to the Wroxhams' house, Jane and David sat in front, and Mary sat behind with the children. The unequivocal warmth of the whole family's welcome, and the still unaccustomed pleasure of having David's arm round her shoulders, made Jane feel so buoyantly happy that it would not have dismayed her to walk the distance.

However, as soon as they reached the house, Mary insisted on making her relax against the pile of cushions prepared for her on the sitting-room sofa, and the children were sent out to play in the garden while their elders had a quiet glass of sherry before supper.

"When is the wedding to be? Before you go abroad again, presumably?" said Mary to her brother.

"We haven't discussed it yet." Something in his tone made her refrain from pursuing the subject.

After the evening meal, while Mary was putting her youngest son to bed, and Doctor Wroxham was in the garden with the other children, David sat beside Jane on the sofa.

"I'm not an invalid. You don't have to be so gentle with me," she murmured presently.

He laughed, and then his eyes darkened and an instant later he was kissing her as fiercely as he had at Lochmühle; only this time there was nothing to prevent her from responding.

188

When, some time later, he stopped kissing her, she could feel his heart thudding as rapidly as her own. "You're making me forget my good resolutions," he said huskily. "Are you willing to get married at once, Jane?"

"Of course – tomorrow if you wish."

The blaze in his eyes made her tremble, but he drew away and said firmly, "I wish it were possible, but it isn't. I can't break my contract, and you have your finals to take. I think we shall both find it easier to concentrate on work if we postpone the wedding until you've graduated."

"But, David . . . a year . . . *a whole year!*"

"I know: it's a hell of a long time to be separated. But it won't make it any easier if we've just come back from a honeymoon. It will only make it harder, my love."

"I suppose you're right."

"I know I am. Besides, we needn't be apart all that time. If I cut a bit off my present leave, I can probably manage a short break over here at Christmas."

Her face lit up. "Oh, David, that would be wonderful. But what about the fare? Surely it's very expensive? And wouldn't you have to pay for it out of your own pocket?"

He smiled. "My pocket will stand it. Do you realise that you've committed yourself to marrying me without having any idea of my income?"

"I know that you don't squander money, but that you aren't mean with it."

"How did you reach those conclusions?" he asked, with amused curiosity.

"You don't smoke – which I do think is terribly wasteful – and you don't seem to drink a great deal. I knew you were a generous person when you bought me the little wooden farmer's wife at Mürren."

"If you regard that as a generous present, you're very easily pleased," he said dryly.

Her thoughts reverting to their time in Switzerland, Jane said, "David, why didn't you kiss me the night we had dinner

189

at Brienz? I'm sure it was your intention when we set out."

"Yes, it was," he agreed, "and I was about to act on it when that gang of young people arrived on the scene, and reminded me how much older I was."

"Was *that* the reason you didn't? – How absurd! I can see that you might find me too young to be interesting, but why should I mind your being older? You're not too much older."

Mary came in. "David, go and talk to Peter for ten minutes, will you? I want to speak to Jane privately."

When her brother had left them, she said smilingly, "Don't look so apprehensive, Jane. There are no skeletons in the family closet, or none that I know about. I merely want to make a confession. Do you remember when you lost your attaché case on the way to Waldshut? It wasn't stolen. I ditched it."

"You ditched it! Why?" asked Jane, astonished.

"I couldn't bear to see you disguising your good looks with those terrible jumble-sale clothes you used to wear. Also I suspected that *you* wanted to look more attractive, but that you would never admit it. Something drastic had to be done."

When, soon afterwards, Mary called the rest of the children to bed, Doctor Wroxham said he thought it would be a good idea if Jane also had an early night.

"I second that," said David, as she began to protest that she was not tired. "It's been a long day for you, and tomorrow I want to go to Norwich and look at rings. Unless" – a glinting look – "your principles forbid you to wear one?"

Jane laughed and shook her head. She said good night to the Wroxhams, and then looked at David and hesitated. There were still so many things to say.

Reading her mind, he said, "I'll come up in half an hour, and bring you a hot drink."

Presently, sitting up in bed, waiting for his tap on the door, she counted the nights since last she had slept in this room. When David arrived with a beaker of cocoa, she said, "Do you realise it's only twenty-two nights since you and John woke me to say it was time to leave for Yarmouth? And only a little more than a month since you climbed through that window and scared me half out of my wits."

"Are you beginning to wonder if we've known each other long enough to commit ourselves?"

"No, because I think three weeks under canvas are equivalent to three months of ordinary life," Jane replied thoughtfully. "People's characters are far more exposed than usual on a camping holiday. If I hadn't been so intent on trying to resist your physical magnetism, I would have realised much sooner what a strong, good character you had. You see, I've always felt that if love is going to last a long time, it should start with a mental affinity, and that any relationship beginning with a physical attraction was bound to burn out after a time."

"I think a lasting relationship is a combination of both kinds of attraction, Jane," he said seriously.

"Yes, I realise that now. But at first I didn't think we had anything in common mentally. All I knew was that when you looked at me in a certain way, all my bones seemed to melt. It scared me to feel so vulnerable."

"But not any longer?"

"Not any longer. I trust you now," she said simply.

When he had kissed her good night and gone downstairs, Jane slipped out of bed to clean her teeth. Then she turned off the lamp, and lay down, and looked out of the window through which David had entered her life and changed its course.

How dumbfounded Belinda would be, she thought drowsily. Everyone who knew her would be astonished. She still couldn't altogether believe it herself. Her mind went back to their first encounter, and remembering how much she had disliked him she smothered a laugh. *Times have changed, Mr. Carleton. It's only the rather dim men who still prefer featherbrained women.* No wonder he had teased her so unmercifully.

Looking forward to tomorrow more eagerly than ever before, she fell asleep.

Why the smile?

...because she has just received her **Free Harlequin Romance Catalogue!**

...and now she has a complete listing of the many, many Harlequin Romances still available.

...and now she can pick out titles by her favorite authors or fill in missing numbers for her library.

You too may have a **Free Harlequin Romance Catalogue** (and a smile!), simply by mailing in the coupon below.